THIS DIARY BELONGS TO:

Nikki J. Maxwell

PRIVATE & CONFIDENTIAL

If found, please return to ME for REWARD!

(NO SNOOPING ALLOWED!!!☹)

ALSO BY Rachel Renée Russell

DORK DIARIES

Dork Diaries
Party Time
Pop Star
Skating Sensation
Dear Dork
Holiday Heartbreak
TV Star
Once Upon a Dork
Drama Queen
Puppy Love
Frenemies Forever
Crush Catastrophe
Birthday Drama

How to Dork Your Diary
OMG! All about Me Diary!

THE MISADVENTURES OF MAX CRUMBLY

Locker Hero
Middle School Mayhem
Masters of Mischief

Rachel Renée Russell

DORK diaries

SPECTACULAR SUPERSTAR!

With Nikki Russell and Erin Russell

SIMON & SCHUSTER

First published in Great Britain in 2019 by Simon & Schuster UK Ltd
A CBS COMPANY

First published in the USA in 2019 as *Dork Diaries: Tales from a Not-So-Best Friend Forever* by Aladdin, an imprint of Simon & Schuster Children's Publishing Division.

Series design by Lisa Vega
The text of this book was set in Skippy Sharp

1 3 5 7 9 10 8 6 4 2

Simon & Schuster UK Ltd
1st Floor, 222 Gray's Inn Road
London WC1X 8HB

Simon & Schuster Australia, Sydney
Simon & Schuster India, New Delhi

A CIP catalogue record for this book is available from the British Library.

HB ISBN: 978-1-4711-7279-3
Export ISBN: 978-1-4711-7336-3
eBook ISBN: 978-1-4711-7281-6

Printed and bound by CPI Group (UK) Ltd, Croydon, CR0 4YY

www.simonandschuster.co.uk
www.simonandschuster.com.au
www.dorkdiaries.co.uk

To Fariah Marie

Keep dreaming and exploring!
Your creativity and imagination
will take you far!

TUESDAY, JULY 1

I'm going to have the MOST. EXCITING. SUMMER. EVER!! SQUEEEEEEE ☺!!!

I was in my school's talent show last fall, and the judge was Trevor Chase, a music producer who works with all the biggest POP STARS! He's a graduate of my school, Westchester Country Day. And get this! He actually selected ME and my GROUP to be the opening act for the BAD BOYZ, a world-famous boy band!

We'll be joining them on their national tour for one month. It's a DREAM come true! Any minute now Trevor Chase will be calling ME to confirm our spot on the tour! SQUEEEEE ☺!!

So I have my cell phone right here next to me while I'm writing in my— Hey! What the . . . ?!!

OMG! WHERE IS MY CELL PHONE?! IT DISAPPEARED ☹!! THIS IS WHAT HAPPENED NEXT!! . . .

BRIANNA?!
Princess Sugar Plum AND Baby Unicorn

HELLO?! YOU'RE NOT PRINCESS SUGAR PLUM! SORRY, DUDE, WRONG NUMBER!

OMG! PLEASE GIVE ME THE PHONE! THAT'S A SUPERIMPORTANT CALL!
Princess Sugar Plum AND Unicorn

NO! I NEED IT TO TALK TO PRINCESS SUGAR PLUM!

HAND OVER MY PHONE! NOW!

BRIANNA! COME BACK HERE WITH MY PHONE!

NOOOOO!!

Okay, this is REALLY bad!

I can't believe I actually missed Trevor's call. By the time I got the phone back from Brianna, he had hung up!

Trevor wants to set up a meeting with the members of my band and our parents to review the tour schedule and sign contracts! ASAP!

But thanks to my BRATTY sister, Brianna, he'll NEVER call back, because he probably thinks he has the WRONG NUMBER!

OMG! I just had the most HORRIBLE thought! . . .

WHAT IF TREVOR REPLACES US WITH ANOTHER BAND AS THE OPENING ACT ☹?!!

This COULD NOT be happening to me! I was hoping it was just another really bad NIGHTMARE and any minute I would wake up in my bed and it would be over!

But then I realized I was totally overreacting.

I needed to remain COOL and CALM and handle this problem like a MATURE young adult!

I hurried back to my bedroom with my phone. Only this time I LOCKED the door so Brianna wouldn't attempt to SNEAK into my room and totally DESTROY my LIFE! AGAIN ☹!

Then I made a brilliant plan to fix everything, including a backup plan B and an emergency plan C.

STEP 1: Call Trevor Chase, explain that I just missed his call, and let him know how SUPERexcited my band is about the upcoming tour.

STEP 2: Pretend I don't know anything whatsoever about the CRAZY MANIAC who HUNG UP on him!

PROBLEM SOLVED ☺!!

I took a deep breath, gripped my phone, and nervously dialed his number. . .

NO PROBLEM ☺! Now it was time to implement my PLAN B! Just leave a detailed MESSAGE! . . .

NO PROBLEM ☺! Now it was time to implement my EMERGENCY PLAN C! . . .

Have a TOTAL MELTDOWN and ASK that deep philosophical QUESTION young people have struggled to answer since the beginning of time! . . .

JUST GREAT ☹!!

Who could possibly be thinking about a VACATION at a time like this?! Doesn't this man REALIZE that he needs to take care of important business matters before it's too late?! WHERE are his PRIORITIES?!

Unfortunately, unless I somehow get in touch with Trevor Chase really soon, it looks like my band and I WON'T be opening for the BAD BOYZ this summer!

Hey! Maybe it's NOT too late for me to change my mind and go on that PARIS trip I turned down for this band tour. If I'm 3,599 miles away on another continent, I WON'T have to break the very BAD news to my BFFs, Chloe and Zoey, that I've DESTROYED their DREAM of touring with the Bad Boyz!

And if THAT wasn't savage enough, I've RUINED their summer and TRAUMATIZED them for life!!

WEDNESDAY, JULY 2

I called Trevor Chase a dozen times today, but no luck. His voice mail is STILL full!

Part of me is hopeful that everything will work out, while another part of me is already assuming the worst. WHY?

Because my boring life can randomly spiral into a total CATASTROPHE in just minutes!

So I was a little anxious when my crush, Brandon, and I started hanging out more this summer.

Okay, I'll admit it. We really like each other. A LOT ☺!

But that doesn't stop me from stressing out about one day doing something STUPID and accidentally sabotaging our friendship!

Like, what if . . .

I GAVE MY PUPPY (AND BRANDON) A BATH ☹!

I TRIED TO PICK A ROMANTIC AMUSEMENT PARK RIDE THAT WASN'T ☹!

MY CUTE IDEA TO SHARE A HUGE ICE-CREAM SUNDAE TURNED INTO A HOT MESS ☹!

THE *HALLOWEEN PARTY ON ELM STREET* MOVIE I PICKED WASN'T A FUN COMEDY ☹!

ME, STARING AT BRANDON
INSTEAD OF THE FIREWORKS

See what I mean?! I can take a perfectly normal situation and make it EMBARRASSINGLY AWKWARD!

Sure, I walk around with a big smile on my face like I'm in control and everything is just fine! But the world has no idea WHATSOEVER how lost, insecure, and confused I REALLY feel.

YES! I KNOW!

I need to just CHILLAX and stop WHINING about how AWFUL my life is (when in reality I'm actually very lucky)!

I wonder if there's an app for that?!

Like, Stop-the-Whine-'n'-Chill.

I would definitely download it to my cell phone and use it every day!

THURSDAY, JULY 3

I can totally understand why a person might have a messy bedroom. But a FULL voice mail box for days on end is just . . . IRRESPONSIBLE and LAZY!

Unlike the massive amount of time and energy it takes to clean a bedroom, you can sort and delete phone messages while you're lying in bed listening to your FAVE tunes. Don't record executives have ASSISTANTS to take care of this sort of thing?

Anyway, my birthday was last Saturday, and I had a huge pool party! And today I FINALLY got to see the special birthday present from my grandma.

She actually redecorated my bedroom! SQUEEE ☺! The coolest part is a new bench and cushion for a window seat, where I can snuggle up to read a book and write in my diary! Chloe and Zoey were DYING to see my ROOM and all my birthday presents! So I had the brilliant idea to invite them to sleep over (and help me write my thank-you notes)! . . .

THANKS, CHLOE AND ZOEY, FOR THAT SUPERCUTE TEE! IT'S NOW MY FAVE!
PARIS
Thanks!
9:15PM

BAD BOYZ
To: NIKKI

"Don't you just LOVE it, Nikki?! Now all three of us have matching Bad Boyz tees!" Chloe said, admiring my pink glittery shirt. "We can wear them on tour!"

"OMG! Have you heard their newest song?! Listen!" Zoey raved as she blasted "I Love You! (Almost as Much as My Skateboard)" on her cell phone.

Since we were on the subject of the Bad Boyz, this was the PERFECT opportunity for me to do the honest and mature thing and casually mention the slight possibility that, you know . . .

THE TOUR THING IS SO NOT HAPPENING ☹!

But I guess I wasn't feeling very honest or mature right then. It didn't help that Chloe and Zoey were SUPERexcited about the tour and would not SHUT UP about it. And I swear that stupid song was giving me a major migraine.

"I STILL can't believe WE'LL be opening for the Bad Boyz on part of their national tour!" Chloe gushed as she opened her overnight bag. "Take a look at these! I've been collecting dozens of magazine articles about them!" . . .

CHLOE, SHOWING US HER STASH OF MAGAZINES ABOUT THE BAD BOYZ

"NIKKI! ZOEY! I just got a FANTASTIC idea!" Chloe suddenly squealed. "We should read ALL these magazine articles about the band. Then, when we finally meet them, we'll already know practically everything about them!"

"Chloe, I LOVE your idea!" Zoey shrieked. "Let's make a Bad Boyz tour SCRAPBOOK! Then we can add our OWN photos and cool stuff from the tour!"

"We'll CHERISH it for the rest of our lives!" Chloe sniffed and blinked back tears as she clutched the magazines to her chest. "And maybe one day we'll share it with our . . . future CHILDREN!"

JUST GREAT!

Now I felt even more AWFUL ☹!

Because I'd missed one STUPID phone call, now we WEREN'T going to get to meet the Bad Boyz or share the experience with our future children.

Sorry! But I couldn't bring myself to tell Chloe and Zoey the TRUTH and BREAK their hearts like that!

Instead, I did something kind. I made a yummy SNACK of hot buttered popcorn! Then we all flopped across my bed and started thumbing through the magazine articles. . . .

MEET THE BAD BOYZ!

AIDAN CARPENTER

singer and choreographer

NICKNAME: Crash HOMETOWN: Houston, Texas

LIKES: skateboarding, comic books, prank TV shows

DISLIKES: sitting still, being serious, salad, rules

LITTLE-KNOWN FACT: Aidan almost got kicked out of the Bad Boyz when he pulled a prank at their first rehearsal by filling the other guys' water bottles with vinegar. YUCK! Luckily, the guys thought it was hilarious and convinced their manager to let Aidan stay. But now they know better than to leave their water bottles lying around!

FAVE LATE-NIGHT SNACK: french fries

PERSONALITY: Aidan is a total prankster and the goofball of the group. He's most likely to be cracking jokes and distracting his bandmates when they're supposed to be rehearsing. But that's because he picks up choreography faster than everyone else, so he doesn't need as much rehearsal time and gets bored. He took ballet, tap, and jazz at Miss Madeline's School for Dance in Houston, Texas.

WHAT HIS BANDMATES SAY ABOUT HIM: "We think Aidan's pranks come from a deep fear that the world might figure out he's a nice guy and use it against him. Or maybe he's just really, really immature!"

MOST BELOVED POSSESSION: skateboard signed by Tony Hawk

MOST IMPORTANT QUALITY IN A CRUSH: sense of humor!

IF HE WEREN'T A MASSIVE INTERNATIONAL POP STAR, WHAT WOULD HE BE?: "Pro skateboarder."

VICTOR CHEN

singer and rapper

NICKNAME: The Viper HOMETOWN: Miami, Florida

LIKES: dropping sick beats, video games, the Miami Dolphins, ketchup

DISLIKES: cold weather, bananas, getting up early, spiders

LITTLE-KNOWN FACT: Vic won his middle school spelling bee with the word "jararacussu." That's a kind of viper! Hmm . . . wonder if that's how he got his nickname?

FAVE LATE-NIGHT SNACK: nachos

PERSONALITY: Vic is the BADDEST of the Bad Boyz, a real tough guy who never shows his softer side (at least when he's onstage). He hails from the mean streets of Miami (actually, the suburbs, but SHH!, you didn't hear that here). He started his first dance crew when he was nine and has a slick break-dancing move named after him (the Viper).

WHAT HIS BANDMATES SAY ABOUT HIM: "Don't let him fool you. Vic's a teddy bear. Well . . . a teddy bear tough enough to withstand a couple of tornadoes . . . but STILL a teddy bear!"

MOST BELOVED POSSESSION: a leather jacket that belonged to Prince

MOST IMPORTANT QUALITY IN A CRUSH: confidence

IF HE WEREN'T A MASSIVE INTERNATIONAL POP STAR, WHAT WOULD HE BE?: "A race car driver. My first job was in my uncle's auto shop, and I still drop by to mess around with the engines when I'm in Miami."

NICOLAS PEREZ

singer and songwriter

NICKNAME: Romeo HOMETOWN: New York City

LIKES: long walks on the beach, poetry, black coffee, meditation

DISLIKES: sports, dishonesty, marshmallows, TV commercials

LITTLE-KNOWN FACT: Nick loves romantic comedies and cries during sad movies.

FAVE LATE-NIGHT SNACK: pizza

PERSONALITY: Nick is the sensitive artiste of the group, the one most likely to stay up all night discussing philosophy or writing a romantic ballad. Just because he's a little bit emo doesn't mean he can't let his perfectly tousled hair down and have some fun. But his first priority is always making sure YOU'RE having fun. He respects you, girl!

WHAT HIS BANDMATES SAY ABOUT HIM: "Nick is either a hopeless romantic or a savage flirt. He's definitely the most popular with girls. But, secretly, bro still sleeps with a teddy bear! You didn't hear that from us!"

MOST BELOVED POSSESSION: the journal he's currently writing poetry and song lyrics in

MOST IMPORTANT QUALITY IN A CRUSH: a beautiful soul

IF HE WEREN'T A MASSIVE INTERNATIONAL POP STAR, WHAT WOULD HE BE?: "A poet or a volunteer in the Peace Corps, to help make the world a better place. I'd probably also work in my family's pizzeria whenever they needed me."

JOSHUA JOHNSON

lead singer and plays piano and several other instruments

NICKNAME: Teacher's Pet   HOMETOWN: Los Angeles, California

LIKES: dogs, chocolate, scary movies, solving physics problems

DISLIKES: broccoli, crowds (unless he's onstage), clowns

LITTLE-KNOWN FACT: Joshua graduated a year early from high school and got into Harvard right before he was offered a spot in the Bad Boyz! He deferred his acceptance and plans to attend in the future.

FAVE LATE-NIGHT SNACK: brownies and ice cream

PERSONALITY: Joshua is the brains of the group and a real mama's boy. He's kind of an introvert, preferring one-on-one conversations to big parties, and he can make anyone he's talking to feel like they're the most important person in the world. He's a total Ravenclaw, and proud of it!

WHAT HIS BANDMATES SAY ABOUT HIM: "Yo, Josh is stupid smart. The stuff he talks about sometimes! We don't even know, man! We wouldn't be surprised if he discovered a cure for cancer."

MOST BELOVED POSSESSION: a handwritten letter from Dr. Martin Luther King Jr. to his great-grandfather

MOST IMPORTANT QUALITIES IN A CRUSH: honesty and brains

IF HE WEREN'T A MASSIVE INTERNATIONAL POP STAR, WHAT WOULD HE BE?: "Maybe a physician or a university professor. Probably both."

WOW! I'm impressed! I had no idea these guys were SO friendly, talented, and cool!

Since I'm a pretty good artist, Chloe and Zoey begged me to start work on our scrapbook. So every day I'm going to read through the magazine articles, pick the best one, and design an awesome scrapbook page.

This project is going to be REALLY FUN ☺!

And possibly a TOTAL WASTE OF TIME ☹!

I was about to spill my guts and tell Chloe and Zoey the TRUTH when another idea about how I could contact Trevor popped into my head.

It was SO simple, I couldn't figure out WHY I hadn't thought of it earlier! Because Chloe and Zoey were close by, I casually picked up my cell phone and pretended to be checking out the Bad Boyz on social media for cool ideas for our scrapbook.

However, since I couldn't get ahold of Trevor by PHONE, I decided to . . .

SEND HIM AN E-MAIL ☺!!

I quickly wrote an e-mail explaining how I'd missed his call and how desperately we STILL wanted to go on tour with the Bad Boyz. When I finally hit the send button, it felt like a ton of weight had been lifted off my shoulders. Trevor always answered my e-mails right away. So I was very sure I'd hear from him within twenty-four hours.

PROBLEM SOLVED ☺!!

What I DIDN'T expect was to hear from him within TWENTY-FOUR SECONDS!

My heart was pounding as I NERVOUSLY opened his e-mail. When Trevor couldn't reach ME by phone, maybe he'd anxiously waited for me to contact HIM via E-MAIL since he'd responded so quickly!!

RIGHT ☺?! WRONG ☹!! . . .

This is what I received. . . .

* * * * * * * * * * * * * * *

Thank you for your recent e-mail. I'm currently out of the office and will be returning later next week. I will respond to your e-mail at that time.

Best regards,
Trevor Chase
(This is an out-of-office automatic reply.)

* * * * * * * * * * * * * * *

AAAAAAAHHH ☹!!

That was me SCREAMING!

But since Chloe and Zoey were in the room, I just did it inside my head so nobody heard it but me.

I CAN'T do this anymore.

I GIVE UP!

FRIDAY, JULY 4

WARNING! This will probably be the LONGEST diary entry EVER!

Today's the FOURTH OF JULY holiday!

And OMG! I've been through SO much DRAMA, it feels like my HEAD is going to EXPLODE into a glittery shower of FIREWORKS!!

A few days ago my parents decided to have a picnic on Lake Wellington on July Fourth.

The area is mostly known for its luxury vacation homes and fancy yachts. And it has a beautiful park that has been open to the public for decades.

But, strangely enough, my dad wanted to go there because of the PEDAL BOATS.

It's this weird boat/bike combo that you sit in and pedal with your feet to make it go.

Dad was SUPERexcited because when he and his brother were kids, they loved to rent pedal boats whenever their family spent time at the park. He said he wanted to continue this wonderful tradition with HIS children.

Personally, it sounded like A LOT of unnecessary work. SORRY! But if I have to be stuck on a boat, I'd rather it be a humongous luxury CRUISE SHIP with a floating water park and zip line! . . .

THIS IS MY KIND OF BOAT ☺!

We arrived at Lake Wellington around noon and had a delicious picnic lunch. But we were a little surprised when ninety uninvited guests showed up. . . .

NINETY UNINVITED GUESTS CRASH OUR PICNIC!

After we finished, my mom put on her noise-canceling headphones to read a book while WE ventured off to rent a pedal boat.

Brianna was fascinated with the boat as soon as she saw it. But I was NOT impressed. Mostly because it was so OLD, it looked like it was probably the SAME one my dad took out when he was a kid.

The boat rental guy started to give us instructions, but Dad interrupted him and bragged that he was a very experienced EXPERT at pedal boats. (Even though he hadn't been in one in thirty years!)

Dad helped Brianna into the boat. But when I stepped forward, he stopped me and made me hand over my cell phone.

"Lake Wellington is a CELL-PHONE-FREE ZONE!!" Dad announced, just as the boat rental guy got a text message.

WHATEVER!

I handed my phone to Dad, and he quickly walked over to where my mom was reading and gave it to her for safekeeping. But I really didn't mind.

I figured I was going to be too busy having fun and pedaling around the lake to text anyone. And I definitely didn't want my phone to get wet.

Finally, Dad, Brianna, and I all got in the boat, and the rental guy shoved us out into the lake.

Brianna was all excited to pedal, so I let her sit in the front with Dad. But she could only reach the pedals if she sat all the way forward on the edge of her seat.

She quickly got distracted, pretending she was Princess Sugar Plum on an exciting ocean adventure, and started singing to the fish.

Really off-key! I bet those fish were happy they didn't have HUGE humanlike ears.

I was kind of enjoying my seat in the back.

If I shut out the sound of my dad huffing and puffing and Brianna's shrieking, it was actually kind of RELAXING out there on the lake. . . .

ME, CHILLAXING IN THE PEDAL BOAT!

Well, UNTIL my dad told Brianna to switch seats with ME so I could help HIM pedal.

"This is A LOT harder than I remembered," he wheezed as I helped Brianna climb into the back. "Thank goodness my strong, powerful daughter is here to help."

Okay, I did feel kind of strong and powerful for about ten minutes. I was making a boat move across a lake, by the power of my legs alone!! (Well, also my dad's legs. But he slowed down a LOT after I took over for Brianna.)

Then, all of a sudden . . . there was a loud THUMP, and my pedals FROZE!! I couldn't move them at all! And when I looked over at my dad, his pedals weren't moving either!!

But that was because he was ASLEEP!!

"DAD?!" I yelled.

I don't know HOW he fell asleep, because Brianna was

still shrieking songs at the top of her lungs right behind us.

I tapped Dad on the shoulder, and he sat upright.

"WOW! Did I just doze off?!" he sputtered. "I guess being out here on this lake is even more RELAXING than I thought it would be."

YEAH, RIGHT! This lake wasn't relaxing. It was EXHAUSTING!

Dad squinted at the shore, which now seemed miles away. "I can't believe we pedaled out this far."

"WE?!" I snorted. But he was right—we were pretty far from shore.

And now the pedals weren't working.

"Dad, I think something is wrong with this boat! For some reason, I can't get the pedals to move!" I complained as I stomped on them.

He frowned and tried his own pedals, but they wouldn't move either.

"Something must have gotten stuck in the propeller thing," he explained.

If the propeller was stuck, that meant . . .
WE WERE STUCK ☹!

Brianna suddenly stopped singing. "Daddy, we aren't moving anymore. Is something wrong?! Is our boat . . . BROKEN?!" she asked, her lip trembling.

"NO!" I said, at the exact same time that my dad said, "YES!"

Brianna was about to go into a full-blown meltdown. And NOT the mild temper tantrum one. But the kind with shrieking, hiccuping, snot, and enough tears to raise the level of the lake.

"But it's just a GAME!" I said in a rush. "We're not REALLY stuck out here. We just have to figure out how we're going to get back to the shore, okay?"

Brianna nodded and seemed convinced. First we tried shouting for help! But, unfortunately, we were so far out on the lake that no one could hear us. . . .

WE TRY SHOUTING FOR HELP!

Suddenly Brianna smiled. "I know how we can get back to the shore! Maybe a family of dolphins will come and rescue us, like in that last Princess Sugar Plum movie!" she exclaimed.

I was VERY sure there wasn't a dolphin in Lake Wellington, let alone a family of them.

"That's right, Brianna! This means you need to be nice and quiet so you don't scare the DOLPHINS when they come to RESCUE us!" I lied.

"REALLY?! There are actually DOLPHINS in Lake Wellington?!" my dad exclaimed, wide-eyed. "I never saw any when I was a kid! This is going to be even more of an adventure than I thought. HEY! I think I see one! Over there! LOOK!"

Dad pointed toward the front of the boat, and he and Brianna excitedly stared at the water.

"DADDY, I SEE IT TOO! WOW! A DOLPHIN!" Brianna squealed.

I couldn't help rolling my eyes.

All I saw was a four-foot-long partially submerged log floating by.

Sorry, but it looked NOTHING like a ten-foot-long, thousand-pound dolphin. . . .

DAD AND BRIANNA SPOT A DOLPHIN?!

"Listen, Dad! We STILL need to figure out how we're going to get back to shore!" I reminded him.

"Well, we could PADDLE! With our . . . ARMS!" my dad suggested.

He knelt down on the seat and leaned way out over the edge of the boat, paddling at the water with his hands.

"I think it's working!" he called over his shoulder. "Nikki, you paddle on the other side!"

This was RIDICULOUS!

There was NO WAY it was working.

But Brianna looked so hopeful. And I was starting to get hot from the sun blazing overhead. So I got down and paddled on the other side.

The edge of the boat was digging into my chest, and I was barely splashing at the water.

Brianna giggled and screeched, "LOOK! THE DOLPHIN IS PUSHING OUR BOAT BACK TO THE SHORE! THANK YOU, MR. DOLPHIN!"

Then she started singing off-key all over again.

But we weren't moving! **AT ALL!**

"DARN IT! If only I hadn't confiscated your cell phone, Nikki!" Dad said, slapping his forehead.

"So we could dial 911 and request an emergency water rescue?!" I asked glumly.

"NO! I could have taken a VIDEO of this DOLPHIN! No one is going to BELIEVE there's a dolphin in Lake Wellington!" Dad chuckled.

Yep, it was SAD but TRUE! I was trapped in a pedal boat with two people who couldn't tell the difference between a log and a huge marine mammal. We were NEVER, EVER going to get back to the shore!

We were going to WITHER AWAY and DIE of heatstroke and starvation on a CRUDDY pedal boat in the middle of Lake Wellington!!

I'd NEVER get my driver's license, attend prom, graduate from high school, or hang out with Chloe and Zoey again!

But the SCARIEST part was that I was so HOT and EXHAUSTED that the stupid floating log was starting to look like a DOLPHIN to ME, too!

"PLEASE, MR. DOLPHIN! COME AND RESCUE US!" I pleaded along with my dad and sister.

I was pretty sure it winked at me.

But, to be brutally honest, things were NOT looking good for us!

☹!!

SATURDAY, JULY 5

Okay, so we were STUCK in the middle of Lake Wellington on a pedal boat that wasn't pedaling!

And it was totally my DAD'S fault since this was all HIS stupid idea!

Anyway, my dad had figured out that the pedals were not working because something had gotten stuck in the boat's propeller, which was located in the water.

"I just need to take a quick look to see what's going on down there," my dad explained.

But when he stood up and leaned over the side of the boat, it suddenly tipped and wobbled.

I lunged to catch Brianna as she lost her balance and teetered near the edge.

Just as I grabbed her, I heard a loud SPLASH!!! We both whirled around and couldn't believe our eyes. . . .

DAD, FALLING INTO THE LAKE!!

Of course I was worried about my dad. But I was even more worried about poor Brianna.

She is a very young child, and seeing traumatic stuff like this could psychologically SCAR her for the rest of her life.

"OH NO!! Daddy's in the WATER!" Brianna shrieked hysterically. "He's going to SCARE away MR. DOLPHIN and RUIN everything!"

Okay, so I was totally wrong about Brianna being psychologically scarred! She was WAY more worried about the dolphin . . . er, I mean the floating log, than her own dad.

Dad came flailing over to the edge of the boat. "I'm okay, I'm okay!"

But Brianna was still upset. "Get back in the boat right now, Daddy! Then our dolphin will come back and rescue us!"

"Listen, girls, I'm going to swim to shore," he explained. "You two are going to stay here and just relax. Once I get back to shore, the boat rental guy and I will come out in another boat to pick you up. Okay?"

I'm not gonna lie, I was VERY skeptical. My dad can't REALLY swim that well. He basically just dog-paddles.

So off Dad went! Even though it was a LONG way to swim . . . er, I mean dog-paddle.

I peered toward the shore, where I could see my mom. But her head was STILL buried in her book.

The chance of her actually seeing any of us was very slim.

I held on to Brianna's arm tightly while she cheered for Dad. "Swim, Daddy, swim! You can do it! Go find our dolphin and tell him I want a ride on his back! Okay, Daddy?"

The LAST thing we needed was another Maxwell toppling into the lake!

After a while Brianna got tired of cheering and slumped down into her seat.

I was afraid she was going to start complaining nonstop about being tired and bored.

But she suddenly squealed excitedly and jumped to her feet, wobbling the boat like crazy.

"We need to be RESCUED! So let's send a message in a BOTTLE!" she shouted.

The only bottle in the tiny boat was my dad's expensive reusable water bottle.

But since he had NOT gotten very far and was already slowing down, I shrugged and muttered, "Okay, Brianna. I think we're going to need all the HELP we can get."

Brianna had a candy wrapper and a crayon in her pocket, so she wrote "SOS" on the candy wrapper, shoved it in the bottle, and then HURLED it into the lake.

Where it BONKED my dad on his HEAD!! . . .

DAD, GETTING ACCIDENTALLY
KLUNKED ON THE HEAD BY BRIANNA
WITH THE WATER BOTTLE ☹!

I am NOT even kidding!!!

"OWW!" he yelped in pain, and flailed around for a few seconds until he spotted his water bottle bobbing on the surface a few feet away.

"GIRLS! Do you realize this thing cost me twenty-eight bucks?" he fumed as he dove after it. "And WHY would I want a drink of WATER?! I'm out here practically DROWNING in it!"

This whole time my mom had STILL not looked up from her book even ONCE!!

And no matter how much we yelled and shouted, she could NOT hear us.

I didn't think things could get any WORSE, but they did. It was quite obvious that my dad was already exhausted from swimming and was NOT going to make it anywhere close to the shore.

Thank goodness he made it to a BUOY that was floating about thirty yards away from our boat.

He grabbed onto that thing in a panic and held on for dear life. . .

DAD, CLIMBING ONTO A BUOY
AND HANGING ON FOR DEAR LIFE!

"Nikki, I don't think Daddy is going to be able to rescue us. Do you?" Brianna asked somberly as she stared at Dad clinging to that buoy and his bottle.

I wanted to LIE and tell her that Dad had stopped and climbed onto that buoy to have a meeting with Mr. Dolphin so they could plan our rescue.

But as clueless as Brianna can be, when it's important, she can almost ALWAYS spot a lie.

"I think Dad's a little tired right now. But don't worry, Brianna. We'll figure something out! We're going to be okay, and so will Dad!" I explained as I gave her a reassuring hug.

Brianna BELIEVED every single word I said.

But, unfortunately, I DIDN'T!

We were DOOMED!!

☹!!

SUNDAY, JULY 6

I expected Brianna to burst into tears. But I didn't give that little pip-squeak enough credit!!

"You know what, Nikki? Daddy IS going to be okay! Because WE'RE going to rescue HIM!!"

JUST GREAT ☹!

The last time Brianna tried to help out, she'd almost given Dad a concussion by klunking him on the head with a designer water bottle.

We were actually pretty darn lucky he was still out there clinging to that buoy!

Brianna looked around to see what was in the boat that she could use for a rescue. But the seats were made of plastic, and there was nothing else in there but us.

She tapped her chin, deep in thought. "Daddy said something was stuck in the propeller thingy, right?"

Brianna had been singing so loud at the time, I didn't think she'd overheard our conversation.

"Um, yeah. . . ." I shrugged.

"Well, WHERE IS IT?!" she asked.

Soon I was dangling off the back end of the boat while Brianna tightly held on to my feet. I waved my hands around wildly, hoping to hit the propeller thingy!!! (Which, of course, I would NEVER have done if the boat had an ENGINE!! Although, if the boat had an engine, we wouldn't be STUCK!!)

I was about to give up when my hand found the propeller thingy!! And right away I felt a crunched-up plastic water bottle stuck in it.

"OMG! I FOUND IT!" I yelled excitedly.

"YAY!" Brianna shouted, and clapped her hands happily.

Which also meant that she let go of my FEET ☹!! . . .

ME, ACCIDENTALLY FALLING INTO THE LAKE!!

I could NOT believe this was actually happening to me. And it was all BRIANNA'S fault!

"NIKKI! Are you okay?!" my dad yelled from his buoy.

"I'm g-good!" I sputtered as I held on to the back of the boat.

"SORRY!!" Brianna smiled and then shrugged like she had nothing WHATSOEVER to do with the fact that I had almost just DROWNED in the lake.

However, being in the water helped me get a closer look at the plastic bottle that was stuck in the propeller thingy.

I pulled really hard on the bottle. But part of the propeller accidentally broke off and made a small crack in the bottom of the boat.

At first I thought it was my imagination. . .

OMG! WAS OUR BOAT SINKING ☹?!

Then Brianna shrieked hysterically. . .

OUR BOAT IS SINKING ☹!

"I think Mr. Dolphin is going to have to RESCUE US after all!" Brianna giggled and clapped her hands.

Brianna and I didn't have a choice but to abandon ship. Thank goodness we had our life jackets on.

"Come on, girls! Just swim over to the buoy and climb on. There's plenty of room. You can do it!" Dad shouted encouragingly.

Brianna and I dog-paddled over to the buoy as our pedal boat slowly sank.

Then the THREE of us hung on for dear life as the buoy bobbed back and forth and back and forth in the water like a demented amusement park ride.

I was forced to ask myself that VERY difficult question each person must answer when, sadly, it appears that LIFE IS OVER! . . .

ARE WE HAVING FUN YET?! ☹!!

MONDAY, JULY 7

The ONLY good thing about being stuck out on the lake was that it immediately put things into perspective.

Suddenly all my big problems seemed really small. You know, like the whole . . .

BAD BOYZ FIASCO!

If I'd had my cell phone, I would have called Chloe and Zoey right then and told them the truth!

I'm very lucky to have such kind, loving, and loyal friends like them, and I totally DON'T deserve them.

I ALSO would have asked my BFFs to call 911 to send out an emergency water rescue team to a buoy in the middle of Lake Wellington!

But, luckily, none of that was necessary. . .

WE FINALLY GET RESCUED!

A guy in a fancy yacht, wearing designer sunglasses, stopped to pick us up! I was SO happy to get off that STUPID buoy. We climbed on board, and he gave us towels, bottled water, and even a tray of fresh fruit.

"I really LOVED those pedal boats when I was a kid!" he laughed. "But now I just come here on vacation whenever I get the—"

The man stopped midsentence and stared at me. Suddenly he gasped. . . .

"NIKKI MAXWELL?! IS THAT YOU?!"

Then he removed his sunglasses and smiled.

OMG! IT WAS . . . TREVOR CHASE!!

WE HAD JUST GOTTEN RESCUED BY TREVOR CHASE, WHO WAS VACATIONING AT LAKE WELLINGTON!!

I could NOT believe he was standing there!

"Nikki, I thought you were in PARIS for the summer!" Trevor exclaimed.

Um . . . NO! I had no idea why he thought that. I grinned sheepishly and waved.

"Well, I'm REALLY happy to see you!" he continued. "I tried calling you a few days ago, but I think I had the wrong number. I hope you're still interested in opening for the Bad Boyz!"

I just kind of shrugged. I was still in SHOCK!

One minute I was stranded on a buoy in the middle of the lake, and the next I was on a yacht, STARING at Trevor Chase STARING at me!

"I know you're scheduled to join the tour in about two weeks, but I'm confident your band will be ready! So, what do you say?" Trevor smiled again.

"Well, actually, um . . . okay! I think going on tour will be . . . interesting," I said, like it wasn't a big deal.

But inside my head I was screaming hysterically and doing my Snoopy "happy dance"! . . .

ME, DOING MY SNOOPY "HAPPY DANCE"

So now it's official! . . .

MY BAND IS OPENING FOR THE BAD BOYZ! SQUEEEEEEEEEEE ☺!!

We'll be meeting with Trevor to review the tour schedule and sign contracts once he finishes his vacation!

Anyway, when we finally made it back to the shore, we were still wet from the lake.

Happy, relieved, and exhausted, we stumbled over to where Mom was still reading, and we collapsed on the blanket. She looked up, surprised to see us, and removed her headphones.

"You're back already? Wow! Time went by really fast. This book is SUPERexciting and quite the THRILLER! I just hope you three didn't get too BORED pedaling around out there on the lake RELAXING."

Then she put her headphones on and went right back to READING!!

OMG!! My mom had no CLUE what we had just been through!

Actually, we were very LUCKY to still be ALIVE!!

But the best part was that Trevor invited my family to DINNER and to watch the Lake Wellington FIREWORKS from aboard his yacht. . . .

Even though my day started out a complete DISASTER, I ended up having a FANTASTIC holiday!

I was very proud of how Dad, Brianna, and I worked together and stayed calm until we finally got rescued!

And, most important, I learned THREE very valuable LIFE lessons from our HARROWING experience. . . .

FIRST, there are no DOLPHINS in Lake Wellington!

SECOND, never give up HOPE, because you sometimes run into solutions to your problems where you'd LEAST expect them.

And THIRD, NEVER get on another PEDAL BOAT AGAIN!!!!

EVER!!

☺!!

TUESDAY, JULY 8

Today we started daily band practices at Zoey's house. Here are the members of our group. . . .

CHLOE, ZOEY, AND I SING!

Several of my other friends are in my band too.

Violet plays the keyboard, Theo plays lead guitar, and Marcus plays bass guitar. . .

VIOLET, THEO, AND MARCUS ARE SUPERTALENTED MUSICIANS!

And finally, my crush, Brandon, plays the drums! SQUEEEE ☺! . . .

BRANDON ROCKS ON THE DRUMS!

The name of my band is . . .

ACTUALLY, I'M NOT REALLY SURE YET!

I know, it's a little weird, right?!

We got that name totally by accident.

When I filled out the entry form for the school talent show, we hadn't chosen a name for our band yet. So in the blank for "Name of Act," I wrote "Actually, I'm not really sure yet."

And it STUCK!

That name has grown on us, and now we LOVE it!

I guess you could say it's as DORKY as we are.

Anyway, we're SUPERexcited about the upcoming tour!

But we're also really nervous. I mean, what if we totally HUMILIATE ourselves and BOMB onstage?!

In front of THOUSANDS of people?!

In CITIES all across the COUNTRY?!

OMG! My LIFE would be RUINED!

I'd have to transfer to a new school and wear a weird DISGUISE, like maybe a cheap wig and fake mustache, to hide my true identity.

Then I'd be even LESS popular than I am now.

☹!

FRIENDSHIP IS FOREVER! FIND OUT WHICH BAD BOYZ MEMBER IS YOUR BFF!

Want to be the envy of all your friends? Want to get the inside scoop on celeb gossip and style secrets? Want advice from a cute guy who has it all?

Take this quiz to find out which Bad Boyz band member will be your new best friend forever! What better person to share your dreams and secrets with than a Bad Boyz BFF?! 😃

1. The first thing I notice when I meet a person is their:

    A) eyes

    B) smile

    C) personality

    D) hair

2. My dream house is a:

    A) castle

    B) beach house

    C) mansion

    D) penthouse

3. My fave type of movie is:

A) a Disney princess movie

B) an animated adventure movie

C) a fantasy movie

D) a superhero movie

4. My fave emoji is:

A) heart eyes 😍

B) winking eye with tongue out 😜

C) laughing-crying 😂

D) sunglasses 😎

5. My fave ice-cream flavor is:

A) strawberry shortcake

B) birthday cake

C) chocolate chip cookie dough

D) cotton candy

6. Which month is closest to your birthday?

A) January

B) October

C) July

D) April

7. What is your fave motto?

A) Make your dreams come true!

B) YOLO! (You only live once!)

C) Be smart! Be kind! Be courageous!

D) Dare to be different!

8. I would best describe myself as:

A) fun, caring, and friendly

B) popular, outgoing, and athletic

C) smart, courageous, and adventurous

D) chic, creative, and trendy

If you picked mostly As:

NICOLAS is your Bad Boyz Best Friend Forever!!! He's the one person who can always cheer you up when you're down in the dumps! He's your perfect BFF because he totally loves the holiday season, just like you, and he knows EXACTLY what to say and when to say it.

When you're super chatty he can talk, like, forever, and when you're not, he doesn't freak out when you have nothing to say. With Nick, there's no such thing as awkward silence! You can sit for hours and not say a word.

Oh, and he's drop-dead gorgeous, so being the best friend that he is, he doesn't mind you hopelessly staring into his dreamy eyes.

This Bad Boy is truly understanding, is very concerned about others, and totally gets your vibe. And since he's such a great listener, he ALWAYS has the dish on celebrity gossip, the latest breakups, and who's into who!

Hey, that's just one of the small perks of a Bad Boyz BFF, but remember: SHHHHH! You didn't hear it from Bad Boy Nick!

If you picked mostly Bs:

AIDAN is your Bad Boyz Best Friend Forever!!! He's your perfect BFF because you'll never be bored when you hang out together! He's your go-to BFF when you need to laugh and to feel better about life!

If there's anything about Aidan that you can predict, it's his UNPREDICTABILITY and SPONTANEITY! This Bad Boy has a wild imagination and is not afraid to chase his dreams, no matter how crazy they seem to others. As a result of Aidan's personality, you feel invincible when you're together, and you're inspired to always go for it!

Others like having him around too, so he's constantly invited to the best parties and is the center of attention wherever he goes. When you hang with this Bad Boy, you'll never miss out on exclusive Hollywood premieres and events.

Aidan's social skills are off the charts, and with his wit and temperament, he can take any crisis and turn it into a full-blown party! And let's not forget, this BFF is super cute, so you're totally obsessed by his killer smile! You can't help but be genuinely happy with Bad Boy Aidan!

If you picked mostly Cs:

JOSHUA is your Bad Boyz Best Friend Forever!!! He is incredibly loyal and selfless and will go to the ends of the earth to ensure that he's the BFF who has your back for LIFE! Joshua is super intelligent and ambitious and can intuitively spot your vulnerabilities to know when you really need his help and when you want a little space to yourself for that needed alone time.

Although this BFF tends to be generally quiet and unassuming, you'd be surprised to know how passionate Joshua is about his friendships, social issues, and how he stays true to his beliefs and can bravely stand up for what's right.

He is a natural born leader and can astutely talk about all kinds of unusual topics. (Yeah, we said "astutely." Your vocabulary will definitely grow with this guy around!) ☺

Like you, Joshua enjoys fun adventures and the summer months along with all their cool activities. He can't wait to spend quality time with you, his new BFF. This dude is charming, crazy handsome, and really talented, and he has a great personality. He can hang out with the rich and famous and still make time for the important things in his life, like being the best Bad Boyz BFF EVER!

If you picked mostly Ds:

VICTOR is your Bad Boyz Best Friend Forever!!! He's original, he's cool, and he's definitely not afraid to take risks. Sure, sometimes acting first and thinking later can be dicey for your BFF, but more often than not, his impulsiveness leads to a once-in-a-lifetime opportunity that you can share together!

Victor is super exciting to be around because he's bold, determined, and always invested in the moment. He appreciates your honesty and friendship, and above all else, he appreciates your fashion sense, style, and confidence.

This BFF will always tell you what he's thinking with a frankness that may occasionally border on "Oh no he didn't!!" Truthfulness is what you'll treasure in this friendship, and because you're not afraid to do YOU, you'll be besties FOREVER!

Bad Boy Victor is perfect for you since he'll have the scoop on the latest trends. He'll give you style advice and secrets from the industry's finest fashion experts, and he'll give you confidence to rock whatever outfit and haircut your heart desires! With this handsome BFF by your side, you'll have the best time EVER!

WEDNESDAY, JULY 9

Exciting news! I got an e-mail from Trevor Chase, and he'll be flying in to meet with us about the tour on Monday.

After we finished band practice, Chloe showed Zoey and me another magazine article about the Bad Boyz.

"Look! These guys even go on vacations together! FRIENDSHIP GOALS! Right?!"

"OMG! Wouldn't it be great if WE could do that?! I'd LOVE to go on a long vacation with you guys! It would be CRAZY FUN!" I giggled.

Suddenly it hit me! "Chloe! Zoey! Wait a minute! This TOUR will be like a VACATION! We'll be roommates! And traveling and hanging out together! RIGHT?!"

"EVERY. SINGLE. DAY!!" Chloe exclaimed.

"I never really thought of it like that! But you're absolutely right," Zoey agreed. "And I bet we'll stay in SWANKY luxury hotels!"

"And eat fancy meals with delicious desserts at five-star restaurants, prepared by famous chefs!" I mused.

"And swim in huge swimming pools! Where waiters serve those fruity smoothie drinks with cute little paper umbrellas in them," Chloe said excitedly.

"What about the spas? We'll relax in Jacuzzis and get mani-pedis!" Zoey sighed.

"I can't wait to go window shopping! Swanky hotels always have shops and boutiques nearby that have the CUTEST stuff!" I squealed.

"And by the time the tour is over," Chloe said dreamily, "we're going to be BFFs with . . ."

"THE BAD BOYZ!" we shrieked, and almost started hyperventilating. We are going to have a BLAST!

However, for ME personally, the most AWESOME and WONDERFUL thing about our tour will be . . .

NO MACKENZIE HOLLISTER ☺!!

I don't have the slightest idea why she HATES my GUTS.

And even though school is out for the summer, she's still trying her best to totally DESTROY my life!

How do I know this?

Trevor Chase said that when he couldn't reach me, he called MacKenzie to get my phone number since her dance group was in the school talent show too.

And get this! . . .

SHE ACTUALLY TOLD HIM I WAS IN PARIS FOR THE SUMMER!!

But that's not even the WORST part!

Being the ruthless SHE-SNAKE that she is, MacKenzie told Trevor that HER dance group could open for the BAD BOYZ instead!

Trevor was seriously considering her offer. Until he spotted me floating in Lake Wellington, hanging on to that BUOY, and rescued me!

MacKenzie is such a PATHOLOGICAL LIAR!

I can't wait to get away from her for an entire MONTH. My life will FINALLY be DRAMA FREE!

Anyway, there's no question about it. My BFFs and I are about to have the GREATEST summer of our LIVES ☺!

And we'll be spending it with the BAD BOYZ!

Based on everything I've ever heard about them, they're the NICEST guys EVER.

This tour is going to be a DREAM come true!

Hey! WHAT could possibly go WRONG?!

☺!!

YOUR DREAM DATE WITH A BAD BOYZ MEMBER!

You've spent plenty of time fantasizing about dream dates with the Bad Boyz! (No shame in admitting it—we've all done it!) This quiz will tell you once and for all what your ULTIMATE dream date would be, and WHICH Bad Boy will be there to share it with you!

Really, though, there are no wrong answers! No matter what you choose, you're going to get a date with ONE of the Bad Boyz!! Lucky YOU!

1. Pick your fave fruit:

   A) pineapple

   B) strawberry

   C) watermelon

   D) grapes

2. Pick your fave color:

   A) brooding basic black

   B) blissful sky blue

   C) razzle-dazzle red

   D) pink passion fruit

3. Pick your fave Bad Boyz song:

A) "Bad, Badder, Baddest"

B) "I'd Give Anything (To Have My Heart Broken by You)"

C) "Don't Play Me Like That"

D) "You 4 Me"

4. Pick your fave way to kill time:

A) hanging out on the Bad Boyz fan site

B) taking selfies

C) playing games on your phone

D) texting friends

5. Pick your fave city:

A) New York City

B) Paris

C) Miami

D) wherever the Bad Boyz are in concert!

6. Pick your dream career:

A) ambassador

B) fashion model

C) airline pilot

D) surgeon

7. How do you want to be remembered?

A) powerful and wealthy

B) thoughtful and artistic

C) kind and loyal

D) brilliant and world-changing

8. Pick your ideal view:

A) city skyline

B) woods

C) beach

D) mountains

If you picked mostly As:

Your dream date is dancing the night away at the hottest club with VICTOR! Of course you'll go straight to the front of the VIP line—no waiting for you!—and you'll be front and center when Vic takes the stage to drop some beats. Hey, maybe you'll join him and drop your own! But most of the night he'll be focused on you, girl. Get your dancing shoes ready!

If you picked mostly Bs:

Your dream date is dinner at a romantic restaurant with NICOLAS! Candles, flowers, soft music, and tons of fairy lights will set the mood for deep conversation and lingering glances. You'll really find out who this Bad Boy is when the mics are off. After dinner, you'll go to a poetry reading, and if you're lucky, Nick might share a verse or two . . . about you!

If you picked mostly Cs:

Your dream date is burgers and mini golf with **AIDAN**! You know how to have a good time, and you deserve a date who'll make you laugh. Aidan is the sportiest of the Bad Boyz, though we have no idea how he does with a putter. We DO know he'll get top scores in the fun department every time. Afterward, fill up on burgers (and we suggest you share a shake)!

If you picked mostly Ds:

Your dream date is volunteering at an animal shelter with **JOSHUA**! Adorable puppies and kittens AND you get to gaze into Joshua's beautiful eyes! What could beat that?! Honestly, we can't think of much that feels better than doing good for someone else, and if the company is A+, even better! Afterward, you'll go browse a local bookstore and discover you're obviously soul mates because you both love the same books.

THURSDAY, JULY 10

I JUST CAN'T TAKE IT ANYMORE! My family is literally driving me KA-RAY-ZEE ☹!!

Brandon and I decided to hang out at my house after band practice today. We planned another doggie obedience training session with my SUPERcute and rambunctious puppy, Daisy.

But before we could get started, my mom invited Brandon (and me) inside for meat loaf DINNER!

I love my parents, but they can be very embarrassing in front of my friends. So I said NO THANKS.

But Brandon accepted her invitation, to be polite!

OMG! I had a complete MELTDOWN during dinner! My dad rambled nonstop about his extermination business, even though we were trying to EAT!

And my mom kept whispering embarrassing things so loudly, I was SURE Brandon could HEAR her! . . .

MOM AND DAD, TOTALLY EMBARRASSING ME IN FRONT OF BRANDON AT DINNER!

The only GOOD thing about dinner was that Brianna WASN'T there to perform her AMAZING FOOD TRICKS that she brags she "made up all by herself."

She was having a sleepover with a friend and had left an hour earlier, thank goodness!

Brianna would have taken a heaping spoonful of meat loaf, mashed potatoes, and green peas, chewed them three times, and then asked Brandon if he wanted to see an AMAZING trick.

And regardless of whether his answer was "yes" or "no," she would have opened her mouth full of half-chewed food as wide as she could and gone . . .

And, depending on how GROSSED OUT Brandon was, he'd probably lose his appetite and stop eating for three days, six weeks, or two years!

Her other amazing food trick was even more rude.

She'd suck Hawaiian Punch through her straw and then dribble it back into her glass through her nose while humming "Twinkle, Twinkle, Little Star."

But today my bratty little sister outdid herself! Brianna managed to totally HUMILIATE me in front of my CRUSH without even being HOME!! . . .

ME, ACCIDENTALLY SLIPPING AND FALLING INTO BRIANNA'S NASTY DOLLY MUD BATH SPA ☹!!

Brandon tried to warn me, but it was too late!

ICK ☹! That mud was SO slippery! Every time I tried to get up, I'd lose my balance and fall flat on my BUTT into that dolly mud bath spa AGAIN!

I felt like I was in a mud-wrestling match and the MUD was winning!

Finally, Brandon came over and pulled me out of the slippery mess while trying to keep a straight face. It was quite obvious he was biting his lip to keep from laughing at me.

Sorry, but I didn't see what was SO funny! I had mud stuck in places I didn't even know mud could ooze into.

Anyway, Brandon is excited about the Bad Boyz tour too.

He said he's bringing his camera and photography equipment to capture our experience. He plans to make a tour photo album! Very COOL ☺!

But Brandon ALSO admitted he's a little worried about his grandparents not having him there at Fuzzy Friends since he has always been around to help.

He has already ordered dog food and supplies, made vet appointments for shots, and set up the community volunteer schedule for the next six weeks! And as soon as his grandparents sign papers to renew their lease for the Fuzzy Friends building, everything will be taken care of until he returns.

I'm SUPERimpressed he has already completed six weeks of important tasks BEFORE going on tour! Brandon is SO mature and responsible! SQUEEE ☺!

Unlike . . . ME ☹! Hey! I haven't even folded and put away my clean laundry from TWO weeks ago yet!

And I STILL haven't thrown away that box of leftover PIZZA currently MOLDING under my BED from that sleepover with my BFFs ONE week ago! EWWW!!

THE BAD BOYZ PICK A PROM DRESS 4 U

1. Pick your fave dessert:

   A) s'mores

   B) brownie

   C) cupcake

   D) ice-cream sundae

2. Pick your Hogwarts house:

   A) Ravenclaw

   B) Hufflepuff

   C) Slytherin

   D) Gryffindor

3. Pick your fave kind of book:

   A) mystery

   B) romance

   C) fantasy

   D) humor

4. Pick your fave Bad Boyz merchandise:

   A) Bad Boyz doggie sweater

   B) Bad Boyz official journal

C) Bad Boyz glitter T-shirt

D) Bad Boyz bike helmet

5. Pick your fave thing to do with BFFs:

A) slumber party

B) makeover

C) spa day

D) shopping

6. Pick your dream pet:

A) golden retriever

B) horse

C) bunny

D) lizard

7. Pick your fave Bad Boyz album:

A) *Bad to the Bone*

B) *Badder Than Ever*

C) *Bad Blood*

D) *Baddest of the Bad*

8. Pick your fave hairstyle:

A) loose, natural waves

B) classic, elegant updo

C) asymmetrical, spiky, and trendy

D) ponytail

If you picked mostly As:

JOSHUA picked this fresh, edgy JUMPSUIT for you to wear to prom!!! WHAT? A prom dress that's not a dress?!?! Hear us out! Jumpsuits have been seen all over Hollywood red carpets lately. They're just as glam as dresses, with a lot more room to MOVE on that dance floor! Shake it, girl!

If you picked mostly Bs:

NICOLAS picked this classically elegant pastel ball gown for you to wear to prom. SWOON!!! You'll feel like Cinderella, except instead of having to run away at the stroke of midnight, you'll dance the night away. (Unless, of course, you've got a curfew!) And because Nick knows what girls want, this dress even has POCKETS!!!

If you picked mostly Cs:

VICTOR picked this super-trendy dress that nails all the best trends of this year's prom season—glitter, off the shoulder, and a high-low hem! Trendy and fun, this dress is for the girl who loves being the center of attention! Get out there in the middle of that dance floor and let all that glitter catch the light!

If you picked mostly Ds:

AIDAN picked this retro 1920s flapper dress! Who knew he had such classy taste? (When asked, he said he likes the fringe, LOL!) This dress makes us want to get out there and do the Charleston! (Ask your grandma—she'll teach you her moves.) This dress might be retro, but your time is RIGHT NOW, and you are going to have the prom of the century!

FRIDAY, JULY 11

I can hardly believe we'll be leaving to go on tour in just SEVEN days!

Since Zoey is SUPERorganized, she suggested that we start packing our suitcases TODAY. We'll be on tour for four weeks and need to bring outfits to wear during the day.

We don't have to worry about the clothing we'll be wearing onstage, since that will be taken care of by our creative director and our stylist.

I'll be the first to admit I'm no FASHIONISTA! I mostly wear SUPERcomfy jeans, shorts, shirts, sandals, and sneakers during the summer.

But Chloe insisted that our summer wardrobe had to be CUTE, CHIC, and STYLISH like all the famous POP STARS. She actually gave Zoey and me a trendy teen mag called *Fab Funky Fashions* to read for trendy clothing ideas.

I ransacked my closet! Then I desperately dragged out a box of school clothes from last year. . . .

ME, DECIDING MY WARDROBE IS NOT CUTE, CHIC, OR STYLISH ☹!

The good news is that the stores at the mall are having huge summer blowout SALES today! So I can pick up some cute outfits for a great price!

I still have all the birthday money that I got, and I have cash hidden in my sock drawer from the doggie snack business Brianna and I started last month.

How we started a doggie snack business is a very long and complicated story that I really don't have time to go into right now.

But Mom has agreed to take over my duties and help out Brianna while I'm practicing with my band and on tour.

Anyway, I plan to go shopping tomorrow to buy some new clothes!

I was looking through Chloe's magazine to get some cool fashion ideas when I came across a SUPERsurprising advertisement about the Bad Boyz!

I tore it out and stuck it inside my diary. . .

ARE YOU AN ASPIRING
SINGER WHO LOVES
THE BAD BOYZ?!
DO YOU HAVE WHAT
IT TAKES TO BE THE
NEXT BAD BOYZ
MEMBER?!
VISIT OUR WEBSITE
FOR MORE INFO
ABOUT OUR OPEN
AUDITIONS FOR ALL
INTERESTED GIRLZ
AND BOYZ!!
BEING BAD
IS SO GOOD!

The information on their website stated that they are seriously considering adding a NEW BAND MEMBER after their tour is finished!!

OMG! I got BUTTERFLIES just thinking about the possibilities! However, I also have to be very honest with myself.

Yes, I really ENJOY music! But my first LOVE is and will always be . . .

ART is my PASSION!!

I don't know if I could LIVE without it!

But hey! Anything is possible!

Maybe deep down inside my tortured artistic soul, an edgy BAD GIRL band member is just waiting to escape into the BAD BOYZ world!

☺!!

THE BAD BOYZ PICK A LIP GLOSS COLOR 4 U

1. Pick your fave flower:

    A) daisy

    B) rose

    C) orchid

    D) iris

2. Pick your fave retro fashion trend:

    A) overalls

    B) flannel shirts

    C) combat boots

    D) leggings

3. Pick your fave school subject:

    A) PE

    B) English

    C) art

    D) science

4. Pick your fave Bad Boyz music video:

    A) "Later, Hater!"

    B) "Hopelessly Addicted to Your Lip Gloss"

C) "Empty Emoji Emotions"

D) "Bad-alicious!"

5. Pick the best phone case:

A) rainbow sparkles

B) happy heart glitter

C) Bad Boyz logo

D) unicorn madness

6. Pick your fave holiday:

A) your birthday

B) Valentine's Day

C) Halloween

D) July Fourth

7. Pick your fave comfort food:

A) french fries

B) fresh strawberries

C) cupcakes

D) cookies

8. Pick your fave animal:

A) kangaroo

B) butterfly

C) bat

D) koala bear

If you picked mostly As: AIDAN has chosen Don't Be Jelly for your luscious lips! This bright red gloss is the color of strawberry jelly (with a sweet strawberry scent, too)! It's sure to make anyone who's NOT kissing your lips TOTALLY jelly!

If you picked mostly Bs: NICOLAS has chosen Fairy Tears for your magical self! On its own or layered over your favorite lipstick, this iridescent, shimmery gloss will cast a spell on everyone who sees you. (But let us assure you: No fairies were harmed in the making of Fairy Tears.)

If you picked mostly Cs: VICTOR has chosen Dead of Night to bring out your inner goth warrior/zombie princess! Black lip gloss is a bold choice for a bold girl (or guy!) who wants to make a statement. Tell the world to read your lips to know exactly who you are!

If you picked mostly Ds: JOSHUA has chosen Petal to the Metal for you! This barely there pink is perfect for the low-maintenance girl who wants to look fresh-faced and just a little bit stepped up from neutral. Your makeup is subtle, but your smarts are not!

SATURDAY, JULY 12

I grabbed the *Fab Funky Fashions* magazine I'd been reading obsessively for the past twenty-four hours, stuffed it inside my purse, and climbed out of the front seat of the car.

"Just give me a call when you're done shopping, sweetheart. And remember our little talk about stranger danger!" Mom yelled out the window as I hurried toward the main entrance of the mall, pretending I didn't know her.

Because of the Saturday sales, the mall was crowded. Dozens of teen girls craned their necks to see what poor girl had just been publicly humiliated by being treated like a five-year-old.

THANKS, MOM ☹!

My FAVE teen shop is Sweet 16 Forever, and I was thrilled to see that everything was 50% off! At these prices, I'd be able to put together a whole new summer wardrobe! SQUEEEEE ☺!

Chloe and Zoey had stayed home to pack. But both were standing by to give me emergency fashion advice via text. The first thing on my *Fab Funky Fashions Must-Haves* list was a cute summer dress with matching jewelry. I was looking at a SUPERcute dress on a mannequin when I heard two very familiar voices.

"OMG, Tiffany! I have NEVER been so completely HUMILIATED in my entire LIFE! I actually told MY dancers and ALL 8,921 of my followers on social media that Mac's Maniacs was going to be opening for the BAD BOYZ! Mommy had contacted the society page, and Daddy had hired a publicist and camera crew. And then Trevor Chase just brutally CANCELED everything with no warning!"

"That's HORRIBLE, MacKenzie! But didn't you say he told you he'd think about it and let you know his final decision? And his final decision was, um . . . NO!"

"So, whose side are you on, anyway, Tiff?! You're supposed to be MY BFF! I cried for THREE whole days! OMG, isn't this dress to die for?" . . .

ME, OVERHEARING MACKENZIE AND TIFFANY TALKING ABOUT THE BAD BOYZ TOUR!

It wasn't like I was eavesdropping on their private conversation or anything!

I mean, how JUVENILE would that be?!

I was just casually chilling out behind that mannequin, peeking at them and totally minding my OWN business!

"Anyway, Trevor told me he chose Nikki's band! Can you believe it?!" MacKenzie ranted. "What a bunch of talentless LOSERS! Well, except for Brandon, of course. He's definitely boyfriend material. I don't know what he sees in Nikki. Although he does have a soft spot for mangy DOGS! That's the ONLY explanation that makes sense to me!"

"I totally agree!" Tiffany giggled. "His best friend, Max, is SUPERcute too. I'd definitely hang out with HIM! They both volunteer at Fuzzy Friends, right?! So why don't we buy these two dresses and then wear them to go VOLUNTEER there too?"

I was so UPSET, I almost accidentally knocked that GIRL right over! The mannequin, NOT MacKenzie!!

WHO would buy cute dresses to volunteer at Fuzzy Friends and then pretend to care about the poor animals, when the ONLY reason they were REALLY there was to FLIRT?! . . .

. . . TWO COLD, HEARTLESS MONSTERS ☹!

"Tiffany, I LOVE that idea! But we have to volunteer next week! Brandon will be going on that tour, and by the time he gets back, Fuzzy Friends will have ceased to exist!"

"You mean the guys will be so obsessed with US, they won't care about Fuzzy Friends anymore?!" Tiffany asked.

"NO! The place literally won't EXIST anymore! It's going to be a PARKING LOT! Daddy says the hospital around the corner wants to expand. And if he can convince the landlord to sell the Fuzzy Friends building to HIM, he can RESELL it to the hospital for triple the price for their new parking lot and make a HUGE profit! Then Brandon will stop WASTING his time with those stupid FURBALLS and FINALLY pay attention to ME!" MacKenzie complained as she slathered on three layers of Rip-Off Ruby Red lip gloss in a nearby mirror.

"Oh, okay," Tiffany said, looking a bit confused. "But if Fuzzy Friends is a parking lot, then WHERE will they put all those poor homeless animals?!"

MacKenzie turned and stared at Tiffany for what seemed like FOREVER.

"Honestly, I'm n-not sure what's g-going to happen to them," MacKenzie stammered tensely.

Then she gazed in the mirror and twirled her hair as an icy smile spread across her face.

"But you know what THAT sounds like?! NOT my PROBLEM!" she said coldly as she slathered on another layer of lip gloss. "OMG! Tiffany, I think I almost CARED! I just SCARED the SNOT out of myself!"

Then both girls laughed at her SICK little joke.

I stayed hidden behind that mannequin, totally in shock over what I'd just heard.

I didn't say a word, but inside my head I was totally FREAKING OUT!

Of course, there was the possibility that MacKenzie was lying!

I mean, the girl actually lies about her lies.

But her father IS one of the wealthiest businessmen in the city.

And he is KNOWN for his SHADY business deals, UNDERHANDED tactics, and unadulterated GREED for MONEY!

OMG! What if Fuzzy Friends really WAS a parking lot by the time we got back from our tour?!

Brandon would be CRUSHED!

And the lives of several dozen helpless animals would be at risk!

There was no way I could go on that Bad Boyz tour knowing what was about to happen!

I needed to stay home and STOP the sinister Marshall "Moneybags" Hollister and his wicked daughter MacKenzie!

I suddenly felt so NAUSEATED, I thought I was going to throw up my breakfast burrito all over the SUPERcute dress that mannequin was wearing!

☹!!

SUNDAY, JULY 13

In my last diary entry, I had just overheard MacKenzie telling Tiffany that Fuzzy Friends was going to be turned into a PARKING LOT!! I needed to know more about her diabolical plan! So I secretly followed them into casual wear.

"MacKenzie, are you STILL planning to AUDITION for that new member spot in the Bad Boyz?! I saw it advertised on TeenTV! Everyone is talking about it."

"That position is already MINE! The Bad Boyz just don't KNOW it yet!" MacKenzie bragged. "One thing is for sure, I am NOT going to waste my time posting an audition video online like a million other WANNABES! I'm going to audition for them in person and DAZZLE them with my fabulousness! Those guys will be begging me to join their band!"

"OMG, Mac! How did you get a live audition?!"

"Actually, I'm STILL working on it! But I always get EXACTLY what I WANT! Including Brandon!"

When she said THAT, I accidentally hit my head on the jeans rack. . . . BANG!! OWW ☹! . . .

MY COVER IS TOTALLY BLOWN ☹!!

Then Tiffany rushed over. I gave 'em both a dirty look and rolled my eyes so hard, I thought they were going to pop out of their sockets like Ping-Pong balls and bounce into the swimsuit section.

"Nikki, I know you're obsessed with me, but this STALKING stuff is getting a little CREEPY!" MacKenzie glared. "Don't HATE me because I'm BEAUTIFUL!"

"I'm sorry to burst your little bubble, but you can REMOVE 99% of your BEAUTY with a wet facecloth!" I shot back. "And I'm NOT stalking you, MacKenzie! I'm just here shopping for some, um . . . jeans, actually!"

I pushed the jeans I was hiding behind out of the way.

Then I picked up a pair of boyfriend jeans and pretended to look at the price tag.

"Wow! These are cute!" I said out loud to myself, trying my best to ignore both girls.

"THOSE are boyfriend jeans!" MacKenzie smirked. "I suggest you try a brand that fits your personal style. Like a tacky pair of I'M-TOO-UGLY-FOR-A-BOYFRIEND polyester stretch pants from the Dollar Store!"

Okay . . . THIS MEANT WAR!!

"Really? It sounds to me like YOU WANT A BOYFRIEND, MacKenzie! And you're so desperate, you're willing to turn Fuzzy Friends into a PARKING LOT to get one!" I fumed as I stared right into her beady little snakelike eyes. "Brandon would NOT consider YOU girlfriend material!"

Tiffany and MacKenzie exchanged nervous glances. They knew I had overheard their conversation!

"Listen, Nikki, I want to audition for the Bad Boyz! And YOU want Fuzzy Friends to stay open, right?! So let's make a DEAL! If you let ME perform with you at your last show AND introduce me to the Bad Boyz, I'll talk to my dad about Fuzzy Friends! It will be OUR little SECRET! DEAL?!"

I just STARED at MacKenzie in disbelief!

HOW could she ask ME to do something so SHADY and DISHONEST?!

"YOU, MacKenzie Hollister, are a dismally vain, self-absorbed blond abyss of seething WRETCHEDNESS!"

I screamed at her in complete disgust.

But I just said that inside my head, so nobody else heard it but me!

"YOU are a conniving, manipulative BLACKMAILER!" I said, seething with contempt.

Then MacKenzie smiled wickedly . . .

ME, TOTALLY IN SHOCK
THAT MACKENZIE IS ATTEMPTING
TO BLACKMAIL ME!!

I got all up in that girl's face like acne and told her EXACTLY what I thought of her little DEAL!

Then I turned around and walked right out of that store! I called my mom to come pick me up from the mall even though I hadn't purchased a thing.

It's now Sunday night, and I still feel HORRIBLE!

I'm sitting in my bedroom STARING at the wall and SULKING ☹!

Which, for some reason, always seems to make me feel better ☺.

Basically, MacKenzie asked ME to be dishonest, deceitful, and disloyal to Brandon, my BFFs, Trevor Chase, and even the Bad Boyz.

Just to help fulfill her SELFISH AMBITIONS!

I already knew what would happen if I AGREED to this deal. MacKenzie would get exactly what she wanted!

And if my friends ever found out I was involved, they would probably HATE me as much as I would HATE myself!

But what if I DIDN'T agree to MacKenzie's deal?!

What would happen to the animals at Fuzzy Friends?!

And, more important, what would happen to BRANDON and his FAMILY?!

Brandon's grandparents own the animal shelter!

And MacKenzie's dad has a scheme to make sure their lease WON'T be renewed so he can buy the building and then sell it to the hospital to expand its parking lot ☹!

I realize there's a chance that everything could work out just fine.

But there's ALSO a chance it could turn into a complete DISASTER!

All that really matters is that I CARE about Brandon. A LOT . . .

There is NO WAY I'm willing to RISK him getting hurt or being forced to move away. So yes! Today at the Sweet 16 Forever shop at the mall, I made a DEAL with the DEVIL!

And she has blond hair extensions, a designer wardrobe, an addiction to lip gloss, and a guest appearance in the final show of the opening act for the Bad Boyz!!

Hopefully no one will find out that I had anything to do with MacKenzie's OUTRAGEOUS plan to SNEAK onstage to perform live for the Bad Boyz and SNAG that new member position in their band.

Hey! She promised it would be OUR little secret!

Trevor will probably be FURIOUS with MacKenzie, especially after he already told her NO!

At least by the time he KICKS me off the tour, it will basically be OVER!

I guess I should be RELIEVED that I only have to deal with MacKenzie for FIVE MINUTES during our FINAL SHOW and not the ENTIRE FOUR-WEEK TOUR!! That would be PURE TORTURE!

OMG! I would rather have my APPENDIX removed with a RUSTY SPOON than have HER on this Bad Boyz tour!!

MONDAY, JULY 14

Trevor Chase flew in today with our creative director and our stylist! So we canceled band practice since we had meetings scheduled for most of the day.

First we were going to discuss our Bad Boyz tour details with Trevor.

Next we were meeting with our creative director regarding music, choreography, and staging for our twenty-five-minute show.

Then we were having a session with our stylist regarding hair, makeup, and stage wardrobe.

And, finally, there was a meeting with our parents.

Trevor decided to divide us into two groups for all the meetings, mostly due to the wardrobe discussions.

So Chloe, Zoey, Violet, and I were in one group, and Brandon, Marcus, and Theo were in the other.

I have to admit, us GIRLS were pretty PUMPED UP about this TOUR thing! . . .

STARTING THE DAY OFF
WITH UNCONTROLLABLE GIGGLING
AND A GROUP HUG!

The meeting with Trevor Chase was a lot of fun, and he made us laugh.

We were each going to be PAID for the four-week tour! Although, to be honest, WE would have PAID the Bad Boyz to open for THEM.

It was A LOT more money than we'd ever imagined! I was pretty sure that it would cover our first year of COLLEGE, which was AWESOME!

While we were on tour, the four of us would be SHARING a two-bedroom suite! We were VERY happy to hear this news!

We were told our creative director was going to be our chaperone. She'd have a room right next door and keep a close eye on us.

If we broke any of the rules in the Bad Boyz Tour Handbook, we would get demerits. Anyone accumulating ten demerits would immediately be sent home!

GULP ☹!

We had to be in our rooms each evening with lights out within thirty minutes of the end of a concert.

Breakfast, lunch, and dinner were provided by each hotel, and we could eat in the restaurant or have room service. VERY COOL ☺!

That was pretty much it!

Along with all the rules and info in the fifty-page Tour Handbook, which Trevor handed to each of us and instructed us to read carefully.

Our next meeting was with our creative director!

We were really excited to finally meet her.

"Girls, I'm happy to introduce this phenomenally talented woman! I'm very sure you've heard of her," Trevor raved as she strode into the room. "She's a world-famous Olympic gold medalist figure skater and the former director of a national ice show! Please say hello to our Bad Boyz tour creative director . . .

". . . MS. VICTORIA STEEL!"

OMG! VICTORIA STEEL?!!

JUST GREAT ☹!!!

She's the CRAZY DRAGON LADY from that disastrous *Holiday on Ice* charity show Chloe, Zoey, and I skated in last December! That woman HATED me so BAD, she'd ordered her SECURITY TEAM to DRAG me off the ice!

Well, okay! I'll admit I didn't want to skate in the rehearsal for the ice show that day, so I'd faked a BROKEN LEG and wrapped it in a cast made from two rolls of toilet paper and duct tape!

But . . . STILL!! Victoria had totally OVERREACTED and threatened to kick Chloe, Zoey, and me out of the ice show!

My BFFs and I just stared at her, SHOCKED and STUNNED! It felt like a very BAD DREAM!

WHAT'S IN YOUR BAG?! ESSENTIALS FOR THE ULTIMATE BAD BOYZ FAN!

Are you the ULTIMATE Bad Boyz fan? If so, you need to be ready for a possible Bad Boyz EMERGENCY at any moment! Here are SEVEN important things a SUPERFAN must ALWAYS carry!

Permanent Marker — What if you're walking down the street and you run into one of the Bad Boyz?! Once you're done fangirling (who are we kidding—you'll never be done!!), you're going to want to get an autograph. So ALWAYS keep a permanent marker with you!!!

Lip Gloss — Obviously, your lips must be kissable AT ALL TIMES! Always keep a tube of your favorite shade and flavor close by in your purse or pocket. And check out our quiz in this issue on which lip gloss color the Bad Boyz would pick for you!!!

Tic Tac Breath Mints — For those unexpected moments when you're up close and personal with your FAVE Bad Boyz member, you want your breath to be minty fresh! These breath mints taste really good too! Consider using them as necessary with the lip gloss mentioned above.

Compact Mirror — We know you ALWAYS look FABULOUS! However, when you finally meet your fave Bad Boyz member, you definitely want to have a mirror handy to make sure every hair is in place, your lip gloss is poppin', and there is no lettuce stuck in your teeth. You can also use the mirror to make sure you're STILL breathing after he invites you onstage to sing with him.

Music and Headphones — No Bad Boyz fan would ever be without her tunes and a way to listen in every situation! (Hot tip: Wireless earbuds make it easier to get away with SNEAKING a listen in math class!)

Diary or Notebook — The best way to record every single exciting detail of the MOMENT you meet your fave Bad Boyz member is to write it all down so you'll remember it FOREVER! Also, you never know when you're going to be struck by inspiration and need to write down some poetry or song lyrics! Nick always carries a journal with him, and YOU should too!

Water — Being the ultimate Bad Boyz fan is HARD WORK!! It's important to stay hydrated so you can always sing, dance, and fangirl to the best of your ability! (And if you want to be an eco-conscious ultimate fan, you can get your very own Bad Boyz water bottle)!

TUESDAY, JULY 15

Victoria Steel was even more GORGEOUS than I remembered! She's in her late twenties and looks like an A-list Hollywood actress, a runway model, AND a pop princess all rolled into one SUPERglam person.

I also noticed two huge men in black suits with earpieces and two stressed-out-looking assistants on cell phones hovering right outside the door.

She STILL travels with her own security detail and entourage.

Victoria smiled at us warmly. "Hello, girls! I'm looking forward to working with you!" she said, giving each of us air-kisses. "I'm here to help turn you into HUGE stars! Dreams DO come true!"

WOW! This new Bad Boyz version of Victoria Steel seemed to be SUPERfriendly!

But after Trevor introduced Chloe, Zoey, Violet, and me, Victoria folded her arms and narrowed her eyes.

"Chloe, Zoey, and Nikki, you THREE look REALLY familiar! Have we met before?" she asked, staring at us suspiciously.

My BFFs and I exchanged nervous glances and just shrugged. There was NO WAY we were going to admit WE were the THREE clumsy CLOWNS who had skated in her *Holiday on Ice* show last December.

OMG! I'd fallen down on the ice so many times during our performance, my BUTT had frostbite!

"Actually, you HAVE seen them before!" Trevor explained. "I sent you a video of their band a few weeks ago for staging ideas."

"Okay, that explains it. My notes are here on my iPad," Victoria said, rummaging through her purse and becoming irritated when she couldn't find it.

"WHERE IS MY iPAD?!" she suddenly screamed at her staff. "I NEED MY iPAD! RIGHT NOW! How can I do MY job if you're NOT doing YOURS?! WHY AM I EVEN PAYING YOU PEOPLE?!!"

They immediately scrambled, frantically digging in purses, bags, and briefcases. And within seconds . . .

. . . THEY EACH HANDED VICTORIA AN iPAD!

One thing was quite obvious: Victoria STILL had

a really bad habit of YELLING and SCREAMING at people! For no apparent reason.

"How many iPads does it take to calm down a diva?" Violet whispered to us. We all tried not to crack up!

"I need the iPad with the ROSE GOLD case!" she shrieked. "NOT the LEOPARD PRINT! NOT the JEWELED one! NOT the SEQUINED one! And NOT the GLITTER one! You people are USELESS!!"

Victoria rolled her eyes in disgust. Then she turned back to us and plastered a fake smile on her face.

"I'm really sorry, Trevor, but it looks like the iPad I need is back at the hotel. So I'll just e-mail everyone my FABULOUS ideas later today."

"That sounds fine, Victoria. Now, how about an update on our social media campaign for our exciting new opening act?" Trevor asked.

WOW! Our band was actually getting our own social media campaign?! VERY COOL ☺!

"Of course! It'll be BIG! It'll be AWESOME! It'll be TRENDY!" Victoria bragged. "And it'll be A LOT of work! So I plan to hire a social media intern to manage the launch and the daily activity online. This person will accompany us on tour and post updates and candid photos in each city."

"Fantastic!" Trevor responded.

Suddenly Victoria glared at her security guys. "Could someone PLEASE get me a bottled water?! WHY do I even have to ASK? And it better be SPRING water in a GLASS bottle at ROOM TEMPERATURE or it's going straight into the TRASH! HURRY UP! Before I DIE of THIRST!"

The men nodded nervously and quickly disappeared on a quest to find the water she had demanded. Then Victoria smiled at us and asked if we had any questions about the tour. But we just sat there anxiously, way too scared of her to ask any. So our meeting was finally over.

"Thank you for taking the time to meet with both

the girls and the guys today, Victoria!" Trevor said. "So, are you heading back to the hotel?"

Victoria glanced at her watch as she slipped on a pair of blinged-out designer sunglasses. . . .

I WAS LOVING VICTORIA'S GLAM STYLE!

"Actually, I'm being honored as Woman of the Year at a luncheon for the Westchester Institute of Fashion and Cosmetology in one hour. I HATE going to these PATHETIC events, and they're a total WASTE of my time! The people are shallow and boring, and the food is so AWFUL, I wouldn't FEED it to my CAT!" Victoria ranted.

OUCH!! That place is owned by MacKenzie's aunt!

Victoria continued. "But there will be TV cameras and a large crowd of my ADORING fans. Otherwise, I wouldn't bother to show up. Well, it was nice meeting you, girls. I'll be in touch!"

Then she strode out of the room with her staffers scampering after her.

"WHERE IS MY SECURITY?! IF I'M LATE FOR THIS LUNCHEON, SOMEONE IS GETTING FIRED!" Victoria threatened as the elevator door closed.

It was suddenly so quiet in the room that it seemed like all the air had been sucked out by Victoria's negative energy.

Then Violet said, "If someone gets FIRED, they can just put out the flames with the SPRING water in the GLASS bottle at ROOM TEMPERATURE!"

Finally, Trevor cleared his throat. "Well, as you can see, Victoria is a little . . . um, high-strung. But that's to be expected with these creative types. If you have any problems with her, just let me know. She's really good at her job! But, I must admit, her people skills are a bit lacking."

Sorry, but Victoria's lack of "people skills" is just the tip of the iceberg. She has a WAY bigger and more complicated problem than that. And I know exactly what it is, based on my very extensive experience with another DRAMA QUEEN (who will remain nameless). . . .

Victoria Steel is a mean, rude, selfish, spoiled DIVA!

But the really SCARY part is that she's going to be our CHAPERONE on the tour ☹!! . . .

MY FRIENDS AND ME, ON LOCKDOWN WITH OUR GLAM PRISON WARDEN, VICTORIA!

It's going to be a VERY. LONG. FOUR. WEEKS!!

WEDNESDAY, JULY 16

Since we'd had a full morning of meetings on Monday, Trevor took us to Queasy Cheesy for lunch. But my friends and I were STILL traumatized by all the DRAMA with Victoria and barely ate a bite!

OMG! My stomach was SO UPSET, I felt like I might throw up at any minute!

Although, to be honest, EVERY TIME I eat the food at Queasy Cheesy, my stomach gets SO UPSET, I feel like I might throw up at any minute!

Our first meeting of the afternoon was with our stylist. This person would be responsible for our hair, clothing, and makeup while we were onstage.

"Girls, we're very lucky to be working with this world-famous stylist and fashion designer." Trevor smiled. "Not only is he a trendsetter, but he's also one of the nicest and funniest people I know. You've probably seen him on television. I'm very thrilled to introduce our Bad Boyz tour stylist . . .

". . . MR. BLAINE BLACKWELL!"

OMG! It was THE BLAINE BLACKWELL!! We were so EXCITED to see him again! Chloe, Zoey, and I absolutely LOVE this guy, and we're

SUPERFANS! He is FAMOUS for his popular television show

Ugly Dress Intervention!

And his new spin-off show

Ugly Feet Intervention!: The Pedicure Police!

We first met Blaine last March at a Bad Boyz concert. It all started when we somehow lost the backstage passes Trevor had given us. So Chloe, Zoey, and I ended up SNEAKING backstage.

That's where we ran into Blaine, who was there to style the opening act, the Dance Divas.

But, for some strange reason, he thought WE were the Dance Divas! How KA-RAY-ZEE is THAT?!

Well, okay! I'll admit WE might have actually TOLD him we were the Dance Divas. But . . . STILL!

Chloe, Zoey, and I got a complete MAKEOVER! And it was AMAZING!! . . .

OUR FAB MAKEOVER AS THE DANCE DIVAS, COURTESY OF BLAINE BLACKWELL! (THIS IS US ROCKING SUPERCUTE WIGS.)

"I'm very happy to meet you, Violet!" Blaine said. "You have such beautiful, DRAMATIC eyes! And Nikki, Chloe, and Zoey, it's wonderful to see you again!" He smiled. "I'm really looking forward to working with ALL of you on this Bad Boyz tour!"

"OMG! We're DYING to work with YOU, too!" my BFFs and I squealed.

"Well, I can see WHY!" Blaine muttered as he took a closer look at our faces. "Just look at those BROWS! It looks like two chubby, extra-fuzzy caterpillars crawled onto your foreheads and DIED!"

Yes, it was TRUE! Our eyebrows were probably a bit bushy and needed a good plucking.

"And those unruly SPLIT ENDS! Girls, have you no SHAME?!" Blaine ranted. "I could dump your heads in a soapy mop bucket and scrub my bathroom floor with that hair!"

Our hair HAS been a bit frizzy and harder to

manage due to the summer heat and humidity.

"And your clothing choices are HIDEOUS!" Blaine shuddered. "WHERE did you find those GHASTLY outfits?! In a DUMPSTER behind a CONDEMNED secondhand clothing store?!"

OUCH! His comments about our SUPERcute outfits were SAVAGE! We just stared at that guy, totally SPEECHLESS!

OMG! It was SUCH an HONOR to get TOTALLY RIPPED APART by the world-renowned fashion designer and stylist BLAINE BLACKWELL!

He made us feel like disgusting, fashion-challenged ZOO ANIMALS ☹!! And we were LOVING it ☺!!

"Okay, Violet gets a pass since she's new to this process. But the THREE of you have been found GUILTY of numerous unspeakable CRIMES against FASHION!" Blaine exclaimed. "I promise to give each of you my very best MAKEOVER! But just remember, girls, I'm a stylist, not a MAGICIAN!"

Next Blaine showed us some sketches of the fashions he'd designed for us to wear onstage. . . .

WE LOVE THE FASHIONS BLAINE DESIGNED JUST FOR US!

Then he evaluated our skin types and special-ordered each of us an expensive cosmetic case of custom makeup colors, including lip gloss ☺!

We had such a BLAST with Blaine that we were a little sad when our session with him was over.

Finally, Trevor met with all our parents. He talked about really BORING stuff and answered a lot of even more BORING questions from parents. Then everyone went into a fancy conference room with a huge table and signed a ton of paperwork.

On the way home, my parents admitted that they were a little nervous about me going on tour.

But I wasn't worried at all! The Bad Boyz is an internationally famous band, and the SECURITY for the tour and concerts is EXCEPTIONAL!

Although, my friends and I won't NEED security. Our chaperone, Victoria Steel, is MEANER and SCARIER than a JUNKYARD DOG!! ☹!!

THE BAD BOYZ PLAN A SURPRISE BIRTHDAY PARTY 4 U!

Your BIRTHDAY only comes once a year! So it's the perfect excuse to invite twenty of your closest friends over and play super-exciting games like Spin the Bottle, Would You Rather, Truth or Dare, and Never Have I Ever! The only problem is that you've never thrown a big bash before, and you're totally clueless about party themes. That's where the Bad Boyz come in! Now you can have a fun and awesome celebration without all the stress!

Take this quiz to discover which Bad Boyz band member is the perfect guy to throw YOUR ultimate SURPRISE birthday party! And find out which exciting theme he's chosen especially for you!

Thanks to your special Bad Boy, friends will STILL be raving about YOUR birthday party at your high school graduation!

1. My fave type of music is:

A) pop

B) hip-hop

C) R & B

D) K-pop/J-pop

2. My fave shoes to wear are:

A) sneakers

B) platforms

C) sandals

D) flip-flops

3. My fave type of pizza is:

A) meat monster

B) loaded with everything

C) cheese

D) Hawaiian

4. My fave phone filter for posting fun pics is:

A) animal ears and glasses

B) crown of flowers

C) heart eyes

D) face swap

5. My fave fun pool float is:

A) dolphin

B) shark

C) flamingo

D) unicorn

6. My fave way to CHILLAX is:

A) read a good book

B) binge-watch my fave show

C) soak in the tub with a bath bomb

D) hang out with friends

7. My fave sundae topping is:

A) hot fudge

B) whipped cream

C) sprinkles

D) gummy bears

8. My fave snack is:

A) cookies

B) nachos

C) popcorn

D) candy

If you picked mostly As:

SURPRISE! Bad Boy **JOSHUA** has planned a **MOVIE NIGHT** party just for you on your birthday!

You are SMART, LOYAL, and SUPPORTIVE, and your friends totally adore you. You enjoy hanging out with them, too. Whether you're watching a hilarious comedy, an exciting adventure, or a spine-tingling thriller, your movie night birthday party will be nonstop fun and GIGGLES! After your scavenger hunt, you and your friends can kick back, chillax, and gossip with the Bad Boyz as you enjoy your favorite movies. Be sure to pop enough popcorn for everyone!

If you picked mostly Bs:

SURPRISE! Bad Boy VICTOR has planned a COSTUME party just for you on your birthday!

You're known for being CREATIVE, TRENDY, and INDEPENDENT. So a costume party will channel your bold fashion sense. Whether it's zombies, pop stars, or superheroes, the stage is set for everyone to have a total BLAST. Generate excitement as you play Truth or Dare, and give out a prize for the most original costume (even though you totally deserve to win it). The Bad Boyz and all your friends will give you a standing ovation for your FABULOUS costume party!

If you picked mostly Cs:

SURPRISE! Bad Boy NICOLAS has planned a PIZZA party just for you on your birthday!

Your friends love you because you're GENEROUS, WARM, and FRIENDLY. And you feed them PIZZA! The Bad Boyz and all your friends will have a BLAST at your pizza birthday party. Using fresh ingredients, everyone will have a chance to make their OWN hot and cheesy pizzas, all while listening to your favorite tunes and playing Spin the Bottle! You can even have a taste-test competition to determine who made the yummiest pizza (even though Nick will slay with his family's secret recipe). Then everyone gets to eat a chewy, gooey slice (or five), making it your BEST birthday EVER!

If you picked mostly Ds:

SURPRISE! Bad Boy **AIDAN** has planned a **POOL** party just for you on your birthday!

Everyone loves hanging out with you because you're OUTGOING, FUN, and have a GOOD SENSE OF HUMOR. It's no wonder your pool party will be a huge SPLASH! Whether you're swimming, munching on yummy grilled burgers, playing Would You Rather, or just floating around soaking up the sunshine, you'll have the happiest birthday EVER! The Bad Boyz and all your friends will always remember your AWESOME party. Don't forget the FLOATIES!

THURSDAY, JULY 17

Tomorrow we leave for the BAD BOYZ tour, and I'm STILL packing my luggage! WHY?!

I finally admitted to Chloe and Zoey that when I went shopping at the mall last Saturday, I was so stressed out, overwhelmed, and anxious, I didn't buy a single thing.

(Of course, I left out a few important details, like how I was STRESSED OUT about MACKENZIE'S ruthless plan, OVERWHELMED with worry about Brandon and Fuzzy Friends, and ANXIOUS about our SECRET deal.)

So I was very surprised when my BFFs showed up today and literally DRAGGED me back to the mall to do some last-minute shopping since that big 50% off summer sale was still going on.

We did several hours of intense power shopping. And when my BFFs finished, I had nine bags and a brand-new, SUPERchic summer wardrobe! . . .

NOW I'M READY FOR THE TOUR!

Chloe and Zoey are the BEST friends EVER ☺!

I only wish they had been shopping with me on Saturday.

The more I think about that little deal I made with MacKenzie, the more I realize how WRONG it was.

I let her MANIPULATE me into doing her EVIL BIDDING by agreeing to let her do a live, onstage audition for the new spot in the Bad Boyz during OUR show.

If Chloe and Zoey find out about it, they're going to be FURIOUS with me!

And if Brandon finds out . . . !!

OMG ☹!

Since all of this directly involves him, his grandparents, and Fuzzy Friends, I wouldn't be surprised if he NEVER spoke to me AGAIN!

And I wouldn't blame him one bit!

I'm trying to help Brandon and save Fuzzy Friends.

But maybe I should just tell my friends, and they can help me do the RIGHT thing.

The good news is that I have almost FOUR weeks to try to figure all this out!

Well, I'm FINALLY all packed and ready to go ☺! . . .

MY SUPERCUTE LUGGAGE FOR THE TOUR!

YES! I realize the hugely dramatic irony that my mortal frenemies, MacKenzie and Tiffany, actually gave me the FABULOUS luggage I'm using for this tour as a birthday gift.

But tomorrow I'll be leaving on the biggest and most exciting ADVENTURE of my ENTIRE life!

And I REFUSE to let ANYONE ruin it!

Not even MACKENZIE!

☺!!

FRIDAY, JULY 18

This is the day I've been DREAMING about for months!!

Today we join the tour as the opening act for the

BAD BOYZ!

SQUEEEEEEEE ☺!! And tomorrow night is our first concert! I'm so excited, I barely slept at all last night.

The first city on our tour is Chicago, Illinois. We received our flight info and itinerary a few days ago with instructions to meet Victoria Steel near our airline customer service desk at 9:00 a.m.

I was nervous about seeing her again. But even my DREAD at having to deal with that bad-tempered ICE QUEEN again couldn't DAMPEN my spirits!

As soon as my parents and I entered the main lobby of the airport, I immediately spotted all my band members gathered near Victoria, who was busy texting. . . .

MY BAND, READY FOR THE WORLD!

I hugged and kissed my family good-bye and promised to call them as soon as I landed in Chicago. I had to break it to Brianna that the Bad Boyz and Trevor fly in a private jet, so she wouldn't get to meet them at the airport. Then my friends and I greeted each other and excitedly chatted about our upcoming tour.

Victoria finally ended her texting convo and motioned for us to gather around. "So! Are you ready to join the Bad Boyz tour?!" she exclaimed.

Of course we all enthusiastically shouted, "YEAH!!"

"GREAT! We're going to check in and head for our gate. But first I have an important announcement! I met a sharp young lady at a luncheon a few days ago. And when I mentioned that I was looking for an intern for my Bad Boyz tour, she generously volunteered for the job. She has extensive experience with social media and her OWN fan base of almost ten thousand followers. I've also heard she's generous, kind, loyal, and one of YOUR BFFs! Perfect! Here she comes now! I'm thrilled to introduce my new social media intern . . .

". . . MACKENZIE HOLLISTER!!"

I could NOT believe my EARS or my EYES!

MACKENIZE HOLLISTER?!!

Our BFF?! We all just stared at her in total shock!

Seeing her was . . . PAINFUL! It felt like I had just gotten HIT in the face! With a BASEBALL BAT!

"Thank you, Victoria! I'm VERY honored to be working with YOU! You're such a wonderful role model for young people today!" MacKenzie gushed as she dramatically placed her hand on her heart. "Hello, everyone! I'm SO happy to be joining you, my BFFs, on this tour as your official director of social media, influencer liaison manager, and peer counselor. As soon as we arrive in Chicago, I'll be holding a meeting to brief you on my expectations and your participation in this campaign. Please be aware that attendance is MANDATORY! So, do you have any questions, concerns, or comments for me?"

I raised my hand. "Um . . . sorry! But I REALLY need to go to the BATHROOM right now!" I muttered as MacKenzie smirked and rolled her beady eyes.

I very calmly walked to the nearest restroom. Then I stepped inside the first stall, locked the door, and . . .

. . . HAD A COMPLETE MELTDOWN!!

I was very UPSET! But at least I handled this situation in a very MATURE and PRIVATE manner. . . .

ME, HAVING A PRIVATE SCREAM FEST!

You DON'T have to remind me! I'm very aware I said, "I REFUSE to let anyone ruin this exciting adventure. Especially MacKenzie!"

WELL! I'm really sorry . . . I LIED! We're going to be STUCK with MacKenzie for the NEXT FOUR WEEKS!! So, as far as I'm concerned, this TOUR is . . .

TOTALLY.

HOPELESSLY.

UNCONDITIONALLY.

RUINED!!

FOREVER ☹!!

The ONLY good thing about this HORRIBLE situation is that it CANNOT possibly get any WORSE!!

EVEN if we LOSE our LUGGAGE and are FORCED to WEAR the exact same FILTHY outfit, socks, and underwear day after day, for FOUR WEEKS straight, without even a TOOTHBRUSH!

EVEN if we're HIT by a two-ton METEOR onstage right in the middle of the chorus of our song, "DORKS RULE!"

ABSOLUTELY NOTHING can be WORSE than MACKENZIE being on this TOUR!!

Thank goodness by the time we landed in Chicago I had calmed down. I was OVER MacKenzie and the fact that she had basically HIJACKED our tour.

My BFFs had convinced me to ignore her and enjoy every second of what was going to be a DREAM come true!

Violet even made me laugh when she made the hysterical joke that MacKenzie would be too busy staring at herself in all the hotel room mirrors to ever go out in public anyway.

And they were right. Our swanky luxury hotel was everything we had imagined, with huge chandeliers, sleek marble floors, and a fountain in the lobby!

Of course we took a few selfies while Brandon took photos of everything for our tour scrapbook.

We were on a tight schedule, so our luggage was sent to our rooms while my band members and I had a lunch meeting with Trevor and Victoria.

MacKenzie conveniently forgot her mandatory meeting and insisted on going straight to her room to get started on her Chicago social media BLITZ.

But I overheard her tell Tiffany on her cell phone that she planned to have a relaxing spa day and order a gourmet meal from room service!

After lunch we had a styling session with Blaine, a wardrobe fitting with our seamstress, and finally, a band practice—complete with a choreographer, who taught us a few new dance moves!

By 4:00 p.m. we were totally exhausted and looking forward to chillaxing in our hotel rooms. That's when Victoria finally told us our room assignments. Chloe, Zoey, and Violet were roommates for the entire tour and sharing a hotel suite. And Brandon, Theo, and Marcus were roommates for the entire tour and sharing a hotel suite.

The Bad Boyz, of course, had a whole wing of the hotel closed off just for them, with security guards stationed at the elevators and the doors to their suites to keep any zealous fans away.

But for ME, there was GOOD news and BAD news!

I'd already come to the conclusion that the GOOD news was that this HORRIBLE tour situation could NOT possibly get any WORSE!! RIGHT?! Well, the BAD news is that I was totally WRONG about the GOOD news!

I was SHOCKED and DISMAYED to discover that MY roommate for the ENTIRE tour is the LAST person on earth I would have chosen. . . .

MACKENZIE HOLLISTER ☹!!

YES! My roommate is MACKENZIE!! There is NO WAY I am going to SURVIVE this four-week tour!

I very calmly walked back down the hall and knocked on my BFFs' hotel room door! And when they answered . . .

. . . I BURST INTO TEARS!!!

All I wanted right then was to go HOME!

!

SATURDAY, JULY 19

SO MUCH happened yesterday that I'll probably be writing about it for DAYS!

Violet was already napping, and the guys had crashed in a room down the hall. Since we didn't want to disturb our bandmates, Chloe and Zoey decided it would be better if I had my NERVOUS BREAKDOWN someplace else. So we took the elevator down to the lobby. I was looking for a private place to dig a deep hole, crawl into it, and DIE, when we ran into Trevor!

Of course we pretended like everything was fine and plastered fake smiles across our faces.

"Hello, girls! Perfect timing!" Trevor exclaimed. "Would you like to meet the Bad Boyz?! I'm on my way to see them right now!"

Did this man just ask us if we wanted to . . .

MEET THE BAD BOYZ?!!

We just stared at Trevor with our mouths dangling open.

"So, I'll take that as a YES!" Trevor laughed.

OMG! We were actually going to meet the Bad Boyz! SQUEEE ☺!!

We took an escalator up to the second floor and walked past four security guards and a half dozen Bad Boyz staff people to a conference room door. Trevor then introduced us to his assistant, Mallory. She told us the Boyz were in the middle of a television interview with TeenTV, but we could watch quietly.

EXCUSE ME, but HOW were we supposed to watch QUIETLY?!! At their last concert, nine girls were rushed to the hospital to be treated for temporary damage to their vocal cords due to excessive SCREAMING!! I reminded myself that the Bad Boyz are humans too! They burp, sweat, and break out with pimples just like the rest of us, RIGHT? WRONG!!

Mallory opened the door to the conference room, and Chloe, Zoey, and I were almost BLINDED by the golden light that flooded out from their angelic GLOW! . . .

OMG! IT WAS ACTUALLY THE BAD BOYZ ☺!!

Well, okay! That glow might have actually been from all the bright lights for the TV cameras!

BUT STILL . . . !

Mallory showed us where to stand in the back of the room. Even though we had to peek around the cameras and lighting equipment, it was quite obvious these Boyz were NOT your average teen guys!

They were sitting in front of a huge backdrop with their latest album cover on it. All of them were gazing intensely at Jade Santana from TeenTV like she was the only person in the whole wide world.

Well, except for Victor, who was wearing shades! So it was hard to tell where he was looking.

But it FELT like he was staring STRAIGHT INTO THE INNER DEPTHS OF MY SOUL!! SQUEEEE ☺!

"OMG! They're even CUTER in person!" Chloe squealed as Zoey and I sighed loudly in agreement.

Mallory shot us a stern look to quiet down.

But Chloe was right! OMG! These boys have perfect eyes, perfect hair, perfect teeth, perfect skin, perfect clothes, perfect . . . EVERYTHING!

"So tell me," Jade said. "You guys are four strong personalities. How do you work so well as a team?"

They all laughed, and I SWEAR even their laughter was in perfect harmony!!

"It's like this, Jade," Joshua said. "When you spend so much time together, you can't help but become one big, happy FAMILY!"

"And you know how ANNOYING family can be!" Aidan smiled as he punched Joshua, and then he threw his arm around his bandmate's shoulder.

Aidan is ALWAYS joking—every Bad Boyz superfan knows that!!

"We all have our strengths," Nicolas said as Zoey

grabbed my arm and tried NOT to pass out. "We're just lucky that our strengths harmonize as beautifully as our VOICES do!"

Zoey is SUCH a NickChick! Even just talking, he sounded as warm and smooth as a pool of melted chocolate! Zoey wanted to dive in and swim around!

"How about you, Vic?" Jade asked, looking toward the end of the row, at the baddest of the Boyz. "How do you feel about making music with these guys?"

We knew what was about to happen! We'd seen it in a million interviews before this one, but never live.

Chloe and Zoey and I grabbed each other and braced ourselves.

Victor sat up, tilted his shades down, and looked straight into the camera. "Jade, what can I say! I'm a member of the Bad Boyz! BEING BAD IS . . . SO GOOD!"

That's when Chloe, Zoey, and I totally LOST IT! . . .

SQUEEEEEEEEEE ☺!!

"That's a wrap!" shouted a producer in a headset.

Instantly the bright lights went dark and the camera crew started packing up the equipment.

Jade ripped off her body mic and gave the Boyz a wave. "Great interview! I've got a flight to catch. I'll see you at the TeenTV Awards next month!"

Soon there was no one else in the room except the Bad Boyz and Mallory, who was checking her phone in the corner. And, of course, US!!

"Should we introduce ourselves?" Zoey whispered.

We all agreed that it was NOW or NEVER! Otherwise, with their SUPERtight security and huge staff, we'd probably only see them as they passed us backstage. Our limited interaction with them over the next four weeks would probably be a quick hello and wave.

But now we had ALL the Boyz to OURSELVES for who knows how long ☺!

Mallory was totally preoccupied at the moment, discussing tour logistics with someone on her cell phone.

We could actually get to know these guys as individuals, not pop stars.

They DO seem SUPERnice!

Hey! Maybe they might even invite us to dinner or to hang out with them!

We could become FRIENDS for LIFE!

"LET'S DO THIS!" I said excitedly.

☺!

SUNDAY, JULY 20

Chloe, Zoey, and I did a quick group hug for good luck!

But before we could take a step toward the Boyz, Joshua stood up and glared at Victor.

"I swear, dude! I'm SO SICK of you saying that CHEESY line, 'BEING BAD IS SO GOOD!' I was about to BARF UP that peanut butter and jelly sandwich I had for lunch!"

Victor spread his arms wide. "Hey! Don't be HATING on me because you're JEALOUS of my SWAGGER, Mr. Smarty-Pants!"

"Dude! How do you even LIE like that, Josh?" Aidan snorted, and then added in a sappy, sweet voice, "We're one big, HAPPY family! And I'm so CUTE and PERFECT, I fart glitter!"

"What was I supposed to say? The TRUTH?!" Joshua shot back. "Aidan is so IMMATURE, we need to hire a NANNY to babysit him on tour so he doesn't poop his pants and pull STUPID PRANKS like TOILET-PAPERING our hotel rooms and putting toothpaste in our shoes!"

"Actually, the TRUTH is that Nick is so STUCK on himself, he KISSES himself good night in the mirror. And he SNORES so loudly, we haven't SLEPT since this tour started!" Victor ranted.

Nicolas laughed sarcastically. "Really?! You want the TRUTH?! Well, MR. TOUGH GUY VIC is a neat freak, a germophobe, and afraid of fuzzy little squirrels!"

Chloe, Zoey, and I just stared at these guys in disbelief as they hurled insults at each other.

"Well, here's MY truth!" Joshua grumbled. "I could be at Harvard instead of wasting my time here with three WANNABE musicians who have a combined IQ lower than a bowl of Cap'n Crunch!"

"Hey, it's not MY fault you dudes have the sense

of humor of a bunch of elderly nursing home patients!" Aidan shrugged.

"Listen, bros! You all need to stop making up LIES about me!" Nicolas exclaimed.

I could see why he would be upset about the mirror thing. I mean, who could be THAT vain?!

"Yes, I SNORE!" Nicolas admitted as his cheeks flushed. "But come on! It's NOT that loud!"

But what about the MIRROR thing?! My BFFs and I had the same exact question: Is it true?!

Victor folded his arms defensively. "I'm NOT afraid of SQUIRRELS! I'm just worried that if I get too close, one might accidentally run up my leg and get tangled in my hair! Wild animals can be VERY dangerous! And they have . . . GERMS!"

Suddenly the guys started yelling at each other like a bunch of spoiled, bratty kids at recess!

YIKES ☹!!

Thankfully, the door opened and Trevor walked in. I was sure he'd be shocked by their behavior! "Okay, guys, listen up!" he said, ignoring the fact that they looked like they were about to have a brawl. . . .

Finally, Trevor sighed in frustration and stepped between the bickering Boyz to separate them. . . .

IT SEEMS LIKE THE BAD BOYZ CAN'T STAND EACH OTHER!

"You need to come up with your final set list for the rest of the tour. We need to prep for the special effects," Trevor continued.

"Let's keep it how it's been for the last nine concerts," Joshua said. "But just add 'Don't Play Me Like That' as the final song."

"Joshua, WHY does it ALWAYS have to be a song YOU wrote?! How about something more EDGY?!" Nicolas said. "Why don't we end with 'Haunt My Dreamz'?"

"Because WE don't want to end with YOU singing another BORING ballad and putting our fans to SLEEP!" Aidan snarked. "There's no energy in that. 'Later, Hater!' is obviously the final number!"

"Dude!" Victor exclaimed. "You just want to end on a DANCE number so everyone can see your TWINKLE TOES while you HOG the stage! Again!"

Trevor sighed. "If your fans ever saw you guys acting like this, your careers would be OVER!! . . ."

That's when Mallory coughed and nodded toward us. "Actually, Trevor, the girls from the opener are here."

Trevor looked from us to the bickering boys. "Well, okay!" He smiled nervously. "I guess it's time for some introductions!"

This was it!

We were finally going to meet the BAD BOYZ!

It was a teenage DREAM!

Although, based on everything we'd just seen, I was VERY worried it was about to turn into a . . .

NIGHTMARE!!

☹!!

MONDAY, JULY 21

We were FINALLY about to meet the Bad Boyz!! I PINCHED myself just to make sure I wasn't DREAMING. . . . OUCH ☹!! YES, I was AWAKE ☺!!

Trevor motioned us up to the front of the room. "Guys, I'd like you to meet members of your new opening act, Actually, I'm Not Really Sure Yet!"

The Boyz turned and stared at us as their frowns and hostility melted into surprise and curiosity. Their moods changed INSTANTLY! All of a sudden they were smiling, friendly, and relaxed.

"Trevor, you're actually NOT really sure about them yet?! Dude, that's just COLD!" Aidan joked. "I think they'll be GREAT as our opening act!"

"Aidan's NUTZ! Just ignore him!" Joshua laughed. "We know that's the NAME of your band. It's cool and very edgy! I like it! So, what's YOUR name?"

I FROZE! Joshua was looking at ME! And smiling! . . .

JOSHUA, SMILING AT ME!! SQUEEE ☺!

Zoey nudged me, but I was totally paralyzed. So she grinned and stepped forward.

"Hi, I'm CHLOE!" she exclaimed. "NO! I mean I'm ZOEY! SHE'S Chloe. That one. Not this one. That's NIKKI! Sorry, I'm a little confused right now. But

I know all the steps to 'I'm So Bad I'm Good.'"

Zoey was a jittery mess! She was smiling really big and not blinking her eyes. At all. She looked like a slightly scary evil CLOWN.

"Okay, Zoey, let's do it!" Aidan said as he busted a move and struck a cool pose. . . .

AIDAN, ASKING ZOEY TO DANCE! SQUEEE ☺!

Aidan took Zoey's hand and spun her around until they were face-to-face. "The first dance break. Five, six, seven, eight!"

Zoey and Aidan danced together like two pros! Then Nicolas and Joshua started singing the song while Vic beatboxed! It was SURREAL!

Everyone clapped when they finished.

"Very smooth moves, Zoey!" Aidan smiled. "I wish we had another serious dancer in the group. Hey, you know we're adding a new member, right?!"

Zoey just stared at Aidan and blushed.

"This is CHLOE!" I said, shoving her forward. "She's a hopeless romantic and loves your ballads!" Chloe stumbled over a chair and fell right into Nick's arms.

I'm so NOT kidding! It was like a scene ripped from one of her favorite teen novels.

"I'M SO SORRY!" she gasped, totally embarrassed.

"Hey! Don't be! You just gave me inspiration for a new song, 'Chloe Fell into My Heart'!" Nicolas gushed as he made a heart sign. . . .

NICOLAS, FLIRTING WITH CHLOE! SQUEEE ☺!

"I'd LOVE to have a new band member help me write ballads!" He smiled.

OMG! Chloe literally turned into a living, breathing HEART-EYES EMOJI!! I thought she was going to fall over and face-plant on the floor.

"How about YOU?" Vic asked, turning to me. "I didn't catch YOUR name. . . ."

VICTOR, ASKING ME MY NAME?! SQUEEEE ☺!

I just stared at him, speechless. "I'm—" I froze. AGAIN! What was WRONG with me?! He asked me my name! It was a simple question! I KNOW my own name!

"I'm—" Now everyone was staring at me!

Okay, I'll admit that I DIDN'T remember my name! But . . . STILL! I had to come up with SOMETHING!!

"I'M . . . a singer and writer!" I blurted out.

"We could always use another lead singer!" Joshua nodded enthusiastically.

"And you write, too! We really need someone to help with lyrics and raps!" Vic added.

"All three of you are SUPERtalented! So are you going to audition to be our new member?!" Aidan asked.

Chloe, Zoey, and I just stared at each other and shrugged.

"Actually, we're not really sure yet!" we muttered nervously.

That's when the Boyz laughed and gave each other high fives!

It took us a moment to realize we'd accidentally said the NAME of our BAND! Just GREAT ☹! But they thought we said it on purpose to be bold and sassy.

"Yeah! We KNOW who you are!" Joshua chuckled.

"Maybe we should try out for YOUR band instead!" Aidan teased.

"Girls run the world, right?!" Nicolas smiled.

"You ladies are FIERCE!" Victor exclaimed.

"Listen, guys!" Trevor said, looking at his watch. "It's almost time for you to do the sound check for your concert this evening. This will be the final night the Dance Divas will be opening for you."

That's when I noticed the guys were whispering to each other.

"Why don't you come hang out backstage at our concert tonight!" they said excitedly.

Chloe, Zoey, and I were too shocked to even answer. . . .

THE BOYZ INVITE US TO THEIR CONCERT!

"Actually, that's a really good idea!" Trevor agreed. "You'll feel a bit more confident if you're familiar with the show! Mallory, please arrange transportation and backstage passes for the girls and their bandmates for tonight's concert!"

The AMAZING thing was that the Boyz seemed to LIKE us! They said they were happy to have us on tour and were looking forward to seeing us later that night.

Then they walked out the door, talking, laughing, and joking with each other like best friends.

That's when I suddenly remembered my name! I ran out into the hall, and just as the door to the stairwell was about to close, I blurted out . . .

"By the way . . .

MY NAME IS NIKKI!

Nicolas stopped in his tracks and spun around.

Then he smiled, stared right into my eyes, and said three SPECIAL words that I'll always remember for the rest of my LIFE!! . . .

HE LIKES MY NAME! SQUEEE ☺!!

"Listen, Nikki, don't tell anyone!" he whispered. "But my name was the same as yours until I joined the Bad Boyz. I was told it wasn't quite BAD enough. So now I'm Nick or Nicolas. But at home everyone calls me Nicky. By the way, I really like your necklace."

"Thanks, Nicolas . . . I mean Nicky!" I smiled. "I actually got it for my birthday. I had a HUGE luau pool party for my birthday last month and invited all my family and friends."

"Do you have any photos?" he asked. "If so, I'd like to see them!"

"Sure! I have dozens!" I took out my cell phone and we scrolled through my party photos.

"WOW! That looks like fun! I wish I could hang out with people like that on MY birthday!" he sighed.

"Why can't you?! Don't pop stars have huge parties with their two hundred closest celeb friends at some swanky club with the paparazzi lined up outside?" I teased. "I always see photos in all the latest mags!"

"It's hard to celebrate birthdays when you're on the road," Nick said. "Most of the time you're so tired, you don't even remember it until Trevor gives you a stale breakfast muffin with a birthday candle stuck in it! Then he sings 'Happy Birthday' really off-key. I mean, just look at these photos! I'd give anything to spend my next birthday with family and friends who really care!"

"Well, why don't you make that a personal goal for your NEXT birthday? Treat yourself!"

"WHAT?! My NEXT birthday?!" he asked, a little bewildered. "I've never actually thought about doing something like that! VERY COOL!"

"Well, it will take some planning! And, of course, you'd have to talk to Trevor and work around your tour schedule. But you should definitely do it if it's important to you and will make you happy!"

"I'm definitely going to take your advice!" Nicolas smiled. "Well, see you tonight, Nikki!"

"Okay! See YOU tonight, Nicky!" I giggled.

Then I wandered back into the conference room with a silly smile plastered across my face.

"Okay, girls! We'll meet you in the lobby in two hours," Trevor said as he and Mallory brushed past me toward the door. "You know the way back to your rooms, right?!"

But he was gone before we could answer.

"OMG! Can you believe we just met the BAD BOYZ and they invited us BACKSTAGE?!" Zoey swooned as she collapsed into a chair.

"Can you believe how AWESOME they were?!" I sighed as I clutched my still fluttering heart.

"Can you believe they asked the THREE of us to AUDITION for their band?!" Chloe squealed as she fanned herself with both hands.

The whole experience was just . . .

UNBELIEVABLE!

Once we'd finally calmed down, Zoey tapped her chin, deep in thought. "Seriously, though, what was up with the Boyz before Trevor introduced us?!"

"Yeah, that was NOT pretty!" Chloe agreed. "Do you think they fight like that all the time?"

"Probably not," I said, giving them the benefit of the doubt. "They would NEVER be able to release all those hit songs and tour together. I honestly think they would have broken up by now!"

"Yeah." Zoey nodded. "Siblings don't always get along either, and that's perfectly normal. Those POOR guys are probably exhausted and stressed out from touring for months on end."

"That makes sense!" Chloe said. "And besides, EVERYONE has a BAD day every now and then!"

As we took the elevator up to our rooms, a tiny part of me wondered how fame and success would impact OUR friendship.

I would HATE to fight like that with Chloe and Zoey! But I quickly dismissed those thoughts. I had REAL problems to worry about.

I was STUCK with MacKenzie as my ROOMMATE for the rest of the tour ☹!

And I totally regretted that stupid DEAL I'd made with her ☹!

But I didn't have time to stress about any of that, either.

In less than TWO hours my BFFs and I were going to be backstage at a concert, hanging out with one of the most FAMOUS boy bands in the world!

SQUEEEEEEEEE!!

☺!

TUESDAY, JULY 22

OMG!! I had dreamed of this moment for months! And now it was FINALLY happening.

It was Friday night, and I was seeing the Bad Boyz LIVE IN CONCERT for the first time!

"The energy is going to be WILD! But just stay calm!" Trevor warned us in the limo. (YES! The LIMO!!!)

I didn't know what he meant until he led us through a long, twisty hallway under the stage and up a flight of stairs.

And there we were! BACKSTAGE in the wings!

Chloe, Zoey, and I were watching the show from the left wing, while Brandon, Marcus, Theo, and Violet were across the stage, watching from the right wing.

The Dance Divas were in the middle of their last show before leaving on a solo tour in Europe.

Onstage, everything was calm and controlled as they danced and sang their biggest hit, "I'm So Over You."

But backstage, it was TOTAL CHAOS!

It seemed like a million people were running around, pulling ropes, moving equipment, placing sets, and pressing buttons. Teams of beefy-looking security guards were stationed at every entrance to the stage.

Trevor introduced us to Sophia, the stage manager. She was wearing all black, standing at a podium thingy, and yelling commands into a headset.

The audience cheered as the Dance Divas finished their final song and bowed.

Zoey had been backstage at mega-concerts before with her dad, so, unlike me, she wasn't all that impressed.

But suddenly she shrieked and grabbed my arm.

The Bad Boyz had arrived backstage!! SQUEEE ☺!!!

The concert was about to start! They gave us big smiles and high fives as they rushed by. . .

WE HIGH-FIVE THE BAD BOYZ
AS THEY GO ONSTAGE!

I thought the audience was extremely loud earlier. But now I was worried the whole stadium was going to collapse as thirty thousand fans completely LOST their MINDS!!

They were standing, screaming, and waving homemade signs declaring their love as the Boyz opened with their huge hit "Bad, Badder, Baddest."

I was worried that my view from backstage wouldn't be that great! But I was WRONG!!

We were SO CLOSE! We could see EVERY STEP and how perfectly synchronized the guys danced!

When the song ended, the screaming got even louder!!

"Hey, Chicago!" Joshua cried. "What's up?!"

In the front row three girls collapsed.

"Code FFF! Three down!" the stage manager shouted. "I repeat, Code FFF! Three down!"

Zoey told me that "Code FFF" meant "Frenzied Fan Fainted"!

Several security guards took off running while medics wheeled out three cots.

"I am SO happy to be in your beautiful city, looking out at your beautiful faces!" Joshua continued over the screams. "And to top it all off, I'm here with my brothers!"

That's when the guys posed just like on the cover of their newest album, with Vic down in front and the others with their arms around each other.

It was FAN-DEMONIUM!!

Next they went into a set of their biggest hits, one right after the other. First "I'd Give Anything (To Have My Heart Broken by You)."

Then "Don't Play Me Like That." Then "You 4 Me."

All the songs sounded even more amazing LIVE!

Then the lights went all blue and moody, and machines started pumping fog onto the stage as Nicolas stepped forward.

"Hey, girl! I LOVE you! I want to sing a few songs just for YOU tonight! Is that okay?!" he shouted as the piercing screams almost shattered my eardrums. . . .

THE GIRLS GO NUTTY FOR NICK!

"Code FFF! Nine down! I repeat, Code FFF! Nine down!" the stage manager yelled into her headset.

OMG!

Those NickChicks were dropping like

LOVESICK FLIES!

After Nicolas sang three love ballads, Vic took center stage for the rap-heavy songs.

Then it was back to more of the biggest hits, with Joshua front and center on vocals and Aidan dazzling the crowd with dance breaks.

And WE were right in the middle of it all ☺!!

Their entire show lasted ninety minutes, which is a very LONG time to sing and dance nonstop!

"This is so AWESOME!" Chloe exclaimed. "Can you believe that WE'RE going to be out on that stage tomorrow night?!"

NO! I could NOT believe it!

The rest of the set was a blur of crazy screaming fans (including me and my BFFs!) and a whirlwind of activity backstage.

That concert was pure Bad Boyz

AWESOMENESS,

from the very first song to the finale!

The final song was also my favorite . . . "Later, Hater!"

It had the same kind of vibe as our song, "Dorks Rule!"

After the concert was over, I introduced Violet, Brandon, Theo, and Marcus to the Bad Boyz.

Everyone was SUPERfriendly and got along really well. All the guys laughed and joked like they'd known each other for years.

Trevor told us the limos had arrived to take us back to the hotel, so we headed out as a group.

But when we passed a drinking fountain, Victor and I stopped to get a drink while the others went ahead.

After we finished, Victor took some lemon-scented hand sanitizer out of his pocket and used it. Then he took an inhaler out of his other pocket and took two puffs.

"These stages and equipment are really dusty, and unfortunately, I'm allergic," he said. "But I try not to make a big deal about it or the guys will tease me. You know, like the SQUIRREL thing!" He smirked.

Victor was the tallest and most muscular, and as a rapper, he had the typical "bad boy" rep.

But when he wasn't clowning around on camera with his bandmates, he actually seemed a bit shy.

Suddenly it made sense to me why he always wore those sunglasses . . . to hide his sensitive side!

"Don't worry about it! Everyone is creeped out by SOMETHING. Personally, I'm afraid of spiders and mean girls slathered in lip gloss!" I joked. "So, have you been around squirrels very much?"

"No, not much at all. But when I was a kid, I saw a horror movie called *Squirrels on a Plane!*" he said.

"Vic, you DO realize that MOST people who saw *Squirrels on a Plane* are afraid of them, right?!"

That's when we both grinned, then snickered, and then snorted with laughter until our sides hurt.

"I've heard that they're not that dangerous as long as there aren't a DOZEN of them! On a plane! You should seriously try feeding just ONE in a park! And work your way up from there." I smiled. "But beware of DUST bunnies! I've heard those little critters can be deadly!"

Victor nodded and gave me a big smile. . . .

VICTOR HAS AN AWESOME SMILE ☺!

"I love your WICKED sense of humor, Nikki! So I'll definitely take your advice!" he laughed as we joined the others. After watching the Bad Boyz onstage and talking to Victor, I was VERY sure the strange behavior we'd seen earlier that day was a fluke!

It was quite obvious that these guys sincerely CARED about each other and were TRUE FRIENDS!

WEDNESDAY, JULY 23

My bandmates and I returned to our hotel, ordered a midnight snack of pizza, and then RAVED about the concert for an entire HOUR!

It was SUPERlate when we finally went to bed.

And we were ALREADY exhausted from our flight to Chicago, styling session, wardrobe fitting, sound check, AND the concert.

My cell phone alarm went off at 5:30 a.m. Saturday morning! But it felt like I hadn't slept at all.

I yawned and opened an e-mail from Trevor titled "Today's Schedule," which had come in an hour earlier, at 4:30 a.m.

WOW! We had an EXCITING day ahead of us that was even MORE hectic than Friday! Every single minute was tightly scheduled until 10:00 p.m.!

We had a breakfast meeting, final wardrobe fitting,

hair and makeup, two-hour photo session with a professional photographer, lunch, dance practice, band practice, sound check at the stadium, dinner, then wardrobe, hair, and makeup AGAIN, and finally . . . OUR SHOW ☺!

WHEW!! Just reading all that made me want to crawl under the covers and go back to sleep.

But since we had a breakfast meeting with Trevor at 6:15 a.m., I dragged myself out of bed.

MacKenzie was still asleep in pink satin pj's with a matching eye mask in the bed across the room.

Even though she'd snagged front-row seats for the tour as the social media intern, she'd thrown a huge HISSY FIT at the concert Friday night when she found out she didn't have backstage privileges or the chance to MEET the Bad Boyz!!

OMG! I felt SO sorry for MacKenzie ☹!

I just LIED! I did NOT feel SORRY ☺! At all!

She actually got into a big argument with the security guards stationed at the stage door and almost got arrested! . . .

MACKENZIE, THROWING A HISSY FIT!

Those guys were hard-core! They didn't care about

her PHONY-BALONEY titles and refused to let her backstage!

After I got dressed, I decided to sneak a peek at MacKenzie's handwritten schedule, which was lying on the desk.

She planned to wake up at 9:30 a.m., have brunch with Victoria at 10:30 a.m., get a mani-pedi at 11:30 a.m., SHOP from 1:00 p.m. to 5:00 p.m., have dinner, and then go to the concert!

So WHEN did she plan to do her JOB as the social media intern and promote our band?! During her BATHROOM breaks?!

My bandmates wanted to sleep as late as possible, so we agreed to meet in front of the hotel restaurant right before the meeting.

I stepped off the elevator and scanned the lobby.

That's when I noticed a teenage guy sitting close by, reading *Skater Life Magazine*. . . .

IT WAS AIDAN!

Two of his security guys were across the room getting coffees.

"Hey, Nikki! What's up?" Aidan smiled.

"It's 6:00 a.m.! Isn't it a little early to be reading a skate mag?" I teased.

"We have an interview on the TV show *Sunrise in Chicago*, and the guys are LATE, as usual. I swear, sometimes it feels like I'm on tour with three brainless, totally exhausted . . . SLOTHS! I'd give anything just to hang out at a skate park again! I guess I really miss my old life and having time to do what I love!" Aidan said wistfully.

I felt sorry for him. "Well, you could always take lemons and make lemonade while you're on tour!"

"Actually, I prefer energy drinks or water when I'm onstage," he muttered as he flipped a page.

"No, Aidan! What I mean is, you travel all over the world, right?! Why don't you visit the BEST skate park in EVERY city on your tour? Even if it's just for a few hours. It would be good exercise and help burn off negative energy!"

Aidan blinked and then stared at me. "I never

thought of that! The best skate parks around the world?! Dude, that's a skateboarder's DREAM!"

One of his security guys interrupted and told him the limo had arrived and the guys were in the elevator on their way down.

"Thanks for the great advice, Nikki!" Aidan said. Then he whispered, "I need to get out to the car first to spread peanut butter on the seats! It'll look like the guys pooped their pants on national TV. It will be my BEST prank yet!"

Then he opened his duffel bag, stuffed his skate magazine inside next to a jar of peanut butter, and left the lobby with his security. Aidan was a hopeless PRANKAHOLIC! I suddenly felt a little sorry for his bandmates.

After our breakfast meeting with Trevor, we were so BUSY, our HEADS were SPINNING! The Bad Boyz had a second show in Chicago later that night. And WE were the OPENING ACT!!

Everyone was unusually quiet on the limo ride over to the stadium for our show. We were about to perform in front of an excited audience of thirty thousand people ☺! And we were NERVOUS WRECKS ☹! . . .

US, TOTALLY STRESSING OUT!

Then Violet said, "Hey, I don't know why we're all so nervous. I mean, I know the thirty thousand fans are there to see us, and don't even care about the Bad Boyz, right?" We all laughed and felt much better.

At 8:00 p.m. sharp, my bandmates and I did a group hug backstage, and then we took our places on the dimly lit stage.

My heart was pounding in my ears as the MC's booming voice echoed through the arena. "Are you ready for a GREAT concert tonight?! This HOT new band's members are BFFs both ON and OFF the stage! CHICAGO, please give it up for . . . ACTUALLY, I'M NOT REALLY SURE YET!!"

Under the blindingly bright stage lights, our fears quickly melted away as we opened with our first number, Queen's "We Will Rock You"!

Chloe, Zoey, and I ran to the edge of the stage and busted a cool hip-hop dance move. *Stomp-stomp-clap! Stomp-stomp-clap! Stomp-stomp-clap!* Violet, Theo, and Marcus joined in on their instruments while Brandon pounded out the ear-popping rhythm on his drums.

"Come on, Chicago!" I shouted. "Get on your feet! . . ."

"And ROOOOCK!!" Chloe and Zoey yelled.

Soon thirty thousand people were on their feet, stomping and clapping to the beat while we belted the song and our band jammed on the music.

OMG! This audience was LOUDER and more EXCITED than the one last night!

We slowed things down and dimmed the lights on our second song. It was the classic all-time favorite, Journey's "Don't Stop Believin'"! Everyone loved that song and clapped along.

"Our final song tonight is one that we wrote," I explained. "It's a reminder to just hang in there even when you feel like you don't fit in!"

The audience roared with excitement and stayed on their feet as we sang our original song, "Dorks Rule!" And by the time we repeated the chorus, thirty thousand voices enthusiastically sang along as the stadium lit up with thirty thousand twinkling cell phone lights.

It was a MIND-BLOWING experience!! . . .

ACTUALLY,
I'M NOT
REALLY
SURE YET!

Chloe, Zoey, and I sang and danced our BUTTS off while Violet, Theo, Marcus, and Brandon played like experienced, professional musicians TWICE their ages.

By the time we finished "Dorks Rule!" the entire stadium was cheering madly.

"Thank you! We LOVE you, Chicago!" Chloe, Zoey, and I said as we smiled and waved.

Then the seven of us lined up and bowed together.

As we left the stage, I felt like I was going to burst into tears from all the energy and excitement.

It was EXHILARATING!

On their way to the stage, the Bad Boyz stopped and gave us high fives.

"You guys were SAVAGE out there!!" they raved.

And they were right!

WE WERE!

At that moment I was SO happy and proud to be a member of the band Actually, I'm Not Really Sure Yet.

But I was even happier and prouder to have them as my FRIENDS!

☺!!

THURSDAY, JULY 24

After our concert in Chicago, MY band was trending nationally on SOCIAL MEDIA!!

SQUEEEEEEEEEE ☺!

Well, okay. We were trending on social media WITH the BAD BOYZ as their cool new opening act! They are ALWAYS trending, especially since they've been on tour.

But . . . STILL!! I was shocked when MacKenzie took credit for it!

And Victoria actually believed her. "MacKenzie, thank you for working countless hours to create an exciting and successful national campaign! This band is very lucky to have a great BFF like you who tirelessly supports them!"

YEAH, RIGHT ☹! As MacKenzie's roommate, I know EVERYTHING she's been doing on this tour: shopping, spa treatments, posting selfies, mani-pedis, lounging by the pool, talking to her friends on the phone, and trying to WEASEL her way backstage to meet the Bad Boyz at concerts!

HOW did I know all of this stuff?! By SNOOPING and reading her SCHEDULE every day!!

MacKenzie hasn't spent ONE SECOND promoting our band on social media! Instead, she's just been promoting HERSELF! I heard her brag to Tiffany that she now has over 150,000 followers on social media since she first announced she was on tour with the Bad Boyz!

MacKenzie is also SUPERmessy and the WORST. ROOMMATE. EVER ☹! I hope I can finish this tour!

Anyway, Sunday morning we left Chicago and flew to Miami for a concert later that night.

Then on Monday we had a concert in Washington, DC, on Tuesday we were in Atlanta, and on Wednesday it was Houston.

By Thursday I didn't have the slightest idea what CITY we were in! I am NOT lying!

I was so mentally and physically EXHAUSTED, I could barely keep my eyes open and my Frappuccino with extra espresso from Starbucks was NOT helping.

Where was I? I saw palm trees, mountains, a beach, and, um . . . a really CUTE GUY waving at me?!

WAIT! THAT WAS JOSHUA!

"Hi, Nikki! Can you talk?" Joshua asked.

"Sure, what's up?" I smiled.

"Well, I just wanted to tell you that your song, 'Dorks Rule!,' is FIRE! I can totally relate to it! Especially the part about NOT fitting in. For most of my life, I've tried really hard. But sometimes it just feels . . . HOPELESS!" he sighed.

"Thanks, Josh! I was inspired to write it by the experience at my school! So I totally get how you feel. Well, kind of. I'm NOT SUPERsmart like you! Well, MOST people aren't SUPERsmart like you."

"So, what am I supposed to do? If I get called Mr. Smarty-Pants just one more time because I want to hang out at the library . . . !!" he muttered under his breath.

"Dork, nerd, geek, freak is all you see . . . ," I began.

Suddenly Joshua smiled. "But just back off and let me be ME!" he finished. "Okay, I get it! It's NOT about trying to make other people like me. I just need to be COMFORTABLE in my OWN skin and like MYSELF!"

"WOW! You really ARE a GENIUS! MR. SMARTY-PANTS!" I teased.

We both laughed at my silly joke. Joshua glanced at his watch. "I'd better get back before security realizes I'm gone! The guys and I have another TV interview in an hour. This circus NEVER ends! I owe you, Nikki. If there's anything I can ever do for you, just let me know."

"Actually, there IS something you can do," I said. "But I feel kind of embarrassed asking!"

"Sure! What is it? And, seriously, you shouldn't feel embarrassed at all," Joshua assured me.

"Um . . . can you tell me what CITY we're in?!"

"Nikki, you're in LOS ANGELES! When you're on tour and don't know what city you're in, that just means you REALLY need some SLEEP!" he laughed. "See you later!"

Okay, THAT made me feel A LOT better.

COOL! I've always wanted to visit Los Angeles!

I was about to head up to my hotel room to try to get some rest before our concert tonight when I got an unexpected text message. . .

IT WAS FROM BRANDON?!!

Our tour schedule has been SO hectic, we've barely had time to talk to each other, let alone hang out. Maybe we could take a walk along that beautiful beach.

His text said . . .

Just got some REALLY bad news from home! Don't know what to do! Where are you?! Need to talk!

I could tell Brandon was really UPSET!

I texted him back . . .

I'm in the Starbucks in the lobby! I'll wait for you here!

I sighed as a wave of DREAD washed over me and my heart started to pound!

Maybe this whole tour thing was a big MISTAKE!

☹!

FRIDAY, JULY 25

I had a sneaking suspicion this emergency meeting had something to do with that little DEAL I'd made with MacKenzie. . . .

And I was ABSOLUTELY right! OMG! Brandon was FRANTIC!!

"Our landlord just sold the building a few days ago, and the new owner is refusing to continue our lease! He wants us out of the building and says by law we have to move in sixty days!"

"OMG! Brandon, that's AWFUL!!" I exclaimed. "I'm really sorry that you and your family are going through all this!"

What was I supposed to say?! . . . "Wow, Brandon! I'm NOT surprised at all! I never expected that SNAKE in blond hair extensions, MacKenzie, to keep her word and honor her side of the deal to get her dad to leave Fuzzy Friends alone if I helped her get onstage with the Bad Boyz!"

"What are we going to do, Nikki?! My grandparents are so upset, they're ready to give up and close Fuzzy Friends. FOREVER! They said they'll both just try to find new jobs! But what about the animals?! I think I need to go home! NOW!"

Brandon looked totally DISTRAUGHT! His face was flushed, his voice was tight, and his eyes were glassy. And it was ALL MacKenzie's FAULT ☹!

"Listen, Brandon! Try not to worry! Okay? We have sixty days to figure all this out, and a lot could happen in that time. And if there's a chance your grandparents might end up unemployed, then the money you're earning on tour will be a really big help! I'll do whatever I can! I promise!"

I purchased an ice-cold bottled water for Brandon. He guzzled the whole thing down in less than a minute, sighed deeply, and gave me a sad smile. Then he apologized for totally losing it and agreed that he needed to finish the tour to help contribute to his family's finances.

By the time Brandon left for drum practice, he was feeling better and was hopeful that things might work out ☺! But I was feeling WORSE ☹! I was MAD at myself and even MADDER at MacKenzie! I was NOT going to let her get away with destroying people's lives.

She started this war, but I was going to finish it! I marched up to our room to confront her. But when I opened the door, I just stared in SHOCK! . . .

OUR ROOM IS A MESS, AND MACKENZIE IS BUSY BLABBING ON THE PHONE!!

"OMG, Tiffany! I have almost 200,000 followers on social media now! Can you believe it? I'm so popular! And I LOVE my new job! I basically just sleep and do whatever I want all day long.

"Have I met the Bad Boyz? Well, not yet. They've been BEGGING me to hang out with them, but I've been SUPERbusy, you know, shopping and stuff. The luggage with more of my clothes arrived today. So I'm ready to grab that new member spot!

"How is the tour so far? It's exciting and so GLAM! The only downside is my roommate, Nikki! OMG! She's a filthy ANIMAL! This place looks like a PIGSTY, and she refuses to clean up after herself. Speaking of PIGS, someone walked in. So I'll call you back later, Tiffany! Toodles!"

"Listen, MacKenzie!" I fumed. "You really need to clean up this place. Our bathroom is just GROSS! Have you been eating chocolate pudding in the bathtub, or is that YOUR muddy bathtub ring?!"

"Nikki, why don't you go crawl back under a rock?!" MacKenzie snarled.

"The only thing crawling in here will be a few dozen ROACHES having a picnic with all the leftover food you have lying around!" I complained.

"Well, I guess I should call YOUR DAD to come SPRAY them!" MacKenzie smirked.

OH NO SHE DIDN'T!! "Actually, that's a good idea!" I shot back. "He's in PEST control and you're a major PEST! He can drop all of you off at the city DUMP! Problem solved!"

"Sorry, Nikki, but can you leave now? Your FACE is giving me stomach cramps, and it's about to turn into a major case of DIARRHEA!"

"NO! I'm not going anywhere until you tell me why YOUR father bought Fuzzy Friends and then refused to renew the lease! You said he wouldn't do it if I helped you audition for the Bad Boyz, and I agreed. So have you FORGOTTEN about our DEAL, or were you just LYING through your teeth?!"

"You're RIGHT! We made a deal. But I changed my mind." MacKenzie shrugged.

"Wait a minute! You DON'T want to audition for the Bad Boyz anymore?!" I asked, surprised.

"Of course I DO! But now I want MORE out of this deal. And YOU'RE going to help ME get it! Or else all those mangy Fuzzy Friends animals will be on the STREET along with Brandon and his family!"

"What else do y-you WANT?!" I stuttered.

"Well, three things, to start! First, I need a backstage pass so I can hang out with the Bad Boyz! Second, you need to introduce me to them as your kind, friendly, and GORGEOUS BFF! Third, you need to start doing social media promo for your band before that witch, Victoria, figures out I've been on vacation the entire tour and FIRES me!"

"You CAN'T be serious!" I exclaimed, stunned.

"One last thing! You need to clean up this FILTHY ROOM! Starting with my nasty bathtub ring! I want to take a strawberry-mango bubble bath, and that tub needs to be spotless! And if you DON'T do EVERYTHING I say, Fuzzy Friends will be a PARKING LOT! Do you understand?!"

JUST GREAT ☹! MacKenzie is a TOTAL SLOB, and just thinking about cleaning up after her made me THROW UP in my mouth a little. . . .

ME, FEELING REALLY SICK!

I STARED right into her cold, beady little eyes!

"MacKenzie, I have just three words for you! GET. HELP. QUICK! Because, girlfriend, YOU'VE LOST YOUR MIND!"

"Actually, I tried to GET HELP! But the front desk said the MAID won't be back to CLEAN again until tomorrow. So now that's YOUR new job, Nikki!"

OMG! MacKenzie was talking so much MESS, I didn't know whether to offer her a breath mint or toilet paper!

In less than one hour, my life has turned into a complete DISASTER! And all I was trying to do was help Fuzzy Friends and Brandon.

But somehow I accidentally created a mean, selfish, lip-gloss-addicted, Bad-Boyz-obsessed . . .

MONSTER!

SATURDAY, JULY 26

Yesterday morning we left Los Angeles and flew to Las Vegas for a concert. Then this morning we flew to Phoenix.

For the past two days, I've been avoiding MacKenzie like the BUBONIC PLAGUE! But she cornered me after lunch today. "Nikki, I'm REALLY looking forward to having a backstage pass for tonight's concert. Otherwise, things could get really UGLY!"

I just rolled my eyes at that girl and was like, "Actually, MacKenzie, things are ALREADY really UGLY! Namely, that FAKE TAN of yours! Have you looked in the mirror lately? It looks like you dipped yourself in a barrel of Cheetos dust! Three times!"

But I just said that inside my head, so nobody heard it but me.

What I REALLY said was, "I'm sorry for the delay, MacKenzie, but I've been trying REALLY hard to get you a backstage pass. But it has to be authorized by the . . . vice president of the record company. And, unfortunately, she's currently . . . on vacation in, um, the . . . Arctic Circle, and her cell phone service is pretty spotty due to all those . . . ICEBERGS and POLAR BEARS. So it's taking a bit longer than I had anticipated."

She actually believed that ridiculous story. But I don't know how much longer this stalling tactic is going to work.

I've managed to avoid cleaning up after her by hanging out in Chloe, Zoey, and Violet's room most of the time.

I was surprised when we got an e-mail from our director of social media/influencer liaison manager/peer counselor and BFF today about a very important meeting she scheduled for 4:00 p.m.

MacKenzie actually wanted US to help with the social media campaign a few hours each day! But this made no sense whatsoever because that job was HERS, not OURS.

Unfortunately, we couldn't attend her meeting because we had a preshow sound check at 3:30 p.m., so I asked her if she would reschedule it.

OMG! MacKenzie TOTALLY LOST IT!! . . .

MACKENZIE, HAVING A MELTDOWN!

Then she started giving out DEMERITS like they were CANDY!

Brandon, Theo, and Marcus got ONE demerit each. Chloe, Zoey, and Violet got TWO demerits each. And I got FIVE demerits! For the same meeting.

But it gets WORSE! MacKenzie gave me another THREE demerits for NOT cleaning up our MESSY room even though SHE made the MESS!

And now if I get TWO more demerits, I could get sent HOME from the tour by Trevor ☹!

I'm sure MacKenzie would LOVE to take my place!

I feel AWFUL that Brandon is having to deal with all this Fuzzy Friends DRAMA while he's on tour. We've been texting each other for the past twenty-four hours, brainstorming ideas for how to save it.

But I might have to tell him the TRUTH about that deal I made with MacKenzie.

I just hope he'll forgive me.

☹!

SUNDAY, JULY 27

After we finished our concert in Phoenix last night, we took a midnight flight to Boston. I barely slept on that long plane ride. I was so EXHAUSTED, I had no idea how I was going to stay AWAKE during our concert tonight!

Once we arrived at our hotel, we had a late breakfast. Then Trevor made a BIG announcement to the Bad Boyz, my bandmates, and me. "Great news! We're going to be doing the biggest concert of our entire tour tomorrow in New York City! And it's going to be FILMED for broadcast on NATIONAL TV at a later date!" he exclaimed.

It wasn't that big of a deal to the Bad Boyz because they've been on television a million times. But it was a REALLY big deal to US! Hey, after this concert we could actually become FAMOUS pop stars! SQUEEEEEE ☺!

My bandmates and I were SUPERexcited and raving about it on the way back to our rooms.

MacKenzie must have overheard us in the hallway or something because as soon as I walked through the door, she started asking me questions about the NYC concert.

"OMG! I can't believe you guys are going to be on NATIONAL television!" MacKenzie gushed. "I've always wanted to be on TV, and I definitely have the pretty face for it! Being seen by millions of people could launch MY career and totally change MY life! You guys are SO lucky!"

"Thank you! We're excited about it too!" I smiled.

Suddenly MacKenzie narrowed her eyes at me. "Now that I think about it, performing at a concert on national TV would be the PERFECT way for ME to audition for the Bad Boyz instead of waiting until your final show! So, Nikki, we need to start planning MY big debut right this minute!"

I gasped in shock! Was MacKenzie actually serious? We glared at each other! Then we had an intense STAREDOWN that seemed to last FOREVER! . . .

MACKENZIE AND ME, HAVING A STAREDOWN

Okay, it was one thing to let her onstage for the LAST ten minutes of our FINAL show at the END of the tour!

But there was NO WAY I was letting her onstage on NATIONAL TV at our BIGGEST concert in the MIDDLE of the tour!

"I'm really sorry, MacKenzie, but I CAN'T do that! It's either the final show like we agreed, or this deal is off!"

"FINE! I'll just call my dad and tell him to move ahead with his plans to make Fuzzy Friends a PARKING LOT!" she snarled. "And it will be ALL. YOUR. FAULT!"

OMG! I was so upset, I wanted to . . . SCREAM!!

I was SICK and TIRED of being manipulated by MacKenzie. And I REFUSED to take any more!

I knew exactly what I had to do!

I took the elevator down to the lobby and found a private spot. Although I was so nervous that my hands were literally shaking, I dialed my cell phone.

"Hello, Trevor! This is Nikki. Would it be possible to meet with you ASAP? I have something I need to tell you, the Bad Boyz, and my band members. And it's not the best news!"

"Well, unless it's an emergency, it will have to wait a bit, Nikki. My schedule for the next twenty-four hours is CRAZY. I'm in a press conference with the Boyz right now. After that I have a meeting with the television producer filming the show in NYC. And, of course, we have the Boston concert tonight."

"I understand that you're SUPERbusy! But all I need is five minutes!" I pleaded.

"Okay, then! I'll give you five minutes. I've already scheduled a meeting tomorrow after lunch to update everyone on our huge NYC concert. But please try not to worry, Nikki! I know this tour schedule is grueling, and you're probably exhausted. But, I assure you, I've been in this business a long time, and what you think is a TOTAL DISASTER is probably at worst a MILD INCONVENIENCE."

"Thanks, Trevor. I just hope you still feel that way tomorrow!" I muttered as I hung up.

I planned to tell everyone at the meeting about that deal I'd made with MacKenzie and how it had ALL gotten out of hand. And then I was going to pack up and go HOME! I was pretty sure I'd be FIRED on the spot, probably by Trevor and definitely by Victoria.

There was also the possibility that Brandon, Chloe, and Zoey would be so ANGRY and DISGUSTED with me, they wouldn't want to be my friends or my bandmates anymore.

Suddenly I got a text message. I assumed it was Brandon, but it was my mom and dad! It said . . .

> SURPRISE ☺! A busload of us parents and local fans are making the trip to NYC tomorrow night for your concert. See you soon! Brianna and Daisy say hi! Hugs and kisses ☺!

JUST GREAT ☹!

Now I was going to be publicly HUMILIATED in front of my PARENTS and an entire BUSLOAD of RANDOM people from my hometown!

Well, at least I'll have a way to get HOME. . . .

ME, TAKING THAT BUS HOME
AFTER I GET FIRED FROM THE TOUR!

My life is so PATHETIC! ☹!!

MONDAY, JULY 28

This morning we took a short flight from Boston to New York City.

Everyone was SUPERexcited about our NYC concert! Except ME ☹. I felt tired, frustrated, and overwhelmed. WHY?

MACKENZIE was getting on my LAST NERVE!!

Even though I had made it perfectly clear I was NOT letting her NEAR the stage, I overheard her on the phone telling Tiffany that she has been practicing THREE dance routines for the THREE songs WE perform in our opening act.

JUST GREAT ☹!

MacKenzie planned to just WALTZ onto the STAGE during OUR performance and basically HOG the ENTIRE show!!

On national television!!

Like, WHO does that?!! She also said Victoria had given her permission to attend an important lunch meeting today with Trevor and the tour talent.

MacKenzie was SO HAPPY she was FINALLY going to meet . . . THE BAD BOYZ!!

And she had planned out every little detail.

First, she was going to wear her most expensive designer outfit, glitter eye shadow, and THREE layers of lip gloss to get their attention.

Second, she was going to take A LOT of photos to post on her social media so she could get even MORE followers.

And third, she planned to start a RUMOR online that she was DATING whichever one of the Bad Boyz let her HUG him in a SELFIE!

I KNOW ☹! I couldn't believe it either! MacKenzie is such a pathological LIAR! . . .

MACKENZIE'S NEW BAD BOYZ BOYFRIEND!

I was actually happy to hear that she was going to be at that meeting.

I planned to EXPOSE all the NONSTOP DRAMA she's been creating in my life, in Brandon's life, and on this tour!

MacKenzie totally deserves to get FIRED from her intern position for not doing her job and to get KICKED OFF this tour for bullying tour members!

I heard Trevor tell Victoria that the NYC concert was so important that he agreed to let the Boyz sleep in until noon so they would be well rested for the TV cameras tonight.

I actually feel sorry for them because I think they're MORE exhausted than I am.

For the past year they've toured Europe, Asia, and the U.S. They usually go to bed after midnight and are up by 6:00 every morning to complete several TV, radio, and magazine interviews by noon. After that they have meetings, practices, recording sessions, choreography, sound checks, and then a concert, with little or no time for themselves.

In spite of being world-famous pop stars, they have very GRUELING lives and not much fun.

Anyway, just in case I got kicked off the tour because of the MacKenzie FIASCO, I decided to send all my band members a text.

I told them that later today I was going to be sharing an issue I had really been struggling with.

And that regardless of what happened, I would always CHERISH their friendship!

I don't think they took me very seriously, because Chloe and Zoey sent me the following text:

> We received your text. But don't worry! Brianna already told us about your hairy legs and crusty eye boogers! We still love you, Nikki!

Then they had the nerve to add a laughed-until-I-cried emoji! HOW RUDE ☹!!

To make matters worse, they also sent that text to Violet, Brandon, Marcus, and Theo!

Yes, Chloe and Zoey are my BFFs, but I did NOT appreciate them putting all my personal BUSINESS in the STREETS like that!

Soon it was 1:30 p.m. and time for our lunch meeting. Everyone met in a conference room for a catered meal of chicken Alfredo.

MacKenzie sat next to Victoria and kept staring at me with her beady little snake eyes!

I was so nervous, I didn't eat a bite. I just pushed my food around on my plate with my fork.

By 2:30 p.m. Trevor was a little concerned that the Bad Boyz had missed lunch. But he told us they were probably having lunch in their rooms.

He said he'd start the meeting as soon as they finished eating and came down.

In the meantime, he turned on the big-screen TV in the room, and the guys decided to watch a baseball game.

By 3:00 p.m. Trevor was worried about the Boyz. He called the head of security and asked him to go to their suites, wake them up, drag them out of bed, and personally escort them down to the meeting.

Victoria reminded Trevor that we had a sound check at the stadium at 4:00 p.m. and were running behind schedule.

So Trevor turned down the sound on the TV, cleared his throat, and started the meeting.

He tapped his watch and reminded me that I only had FIVE minutes.

I stood up as everyone stared curiously at me. I unfolded a letter I had written, took a deep breath, and began reading. . .

ME, READING MY LETTER

I was interrupted by enthusiastic applause from everyone in the room.

I bit my lip and continued. "I'm standing here today because I would like to share some recent experiences that I've had on tour."

MacKenzie's eyes were suddenly as big as saucers, and her cheeks turned bright red.

She took out her phone and starting frantically texting someone. Obviously her BFF, Tiffany!

Just as I was about to continue, I was rudely interrupted. AGAIN!

The head security guy burst into the room, flanked by four other men, and rushed over to Trevor.

"IT'S THE BAD BOYZ, SIR! I'VE GOT SOME DISTURBING NEWS!"

They were all breathing heavily, and their earpieces were dangling below their ears like earrings.

"WE ENTERED THEIR SUITES AS YOU INSTRUCTED, SIR! AND THEY'RE . . . UM . . . MISSING!"

"WHAT DO YOU MEAN, THEY'RE MISSING?" Trevor yelled. "They each have a two-person, twenty-four-hour security team. That's EIGHT highly trained professionals watching FOUR kids! HOW can they be MISSING?!"

"I don't know, sir! But they're NOT in their suites! And the security guards stationed at the elevators didn't see them leave!"

"Nikki, let's put this on hold, please!" Trevor said, motioning for me to sit down.

I sat down. Quickly.

That's when Mallory strode in. "Trevor, the cars are here to transport everyone to the stadium for lights and sound check! It's time to—" She froze and looked around the room, confused. "So, um . . . WHERE are the Boyz?!"

Everyone in the room just kind of looked at each other and shrugged.

I hoped it was just another of Aidan's silly pranks.

But Trevor was LIVID and NOT amused!

We had a sold-out, televised concert in New York City in mere hours!

And the MAIN ACT was missing!!

This DREAM tour was definitely turning into a NIGHTMARE!

☹!

TUESDAY, JULY 29

The Bad Boyz, one of the most famous boy bands in the world, had basically disappeared into thin air!!

Everyone was FRANTIC!!

Trevor called an emergency meeting with the security teams for both the tour and hotel.

Within minutes they scrambled in all directions to check the pool, spa, fitness center, restaurants, and coffee shop for any sign of the Bad Boyz.

Everyone else waited anxiously in the conference room just in case the Boyz decided to show up for the meeting fashionably late. Or with hidden cameras for a live episode of the popular TeenTV show *U Got Pranked!*

Meanwhile, MacKenzie was having a meltdown! She called her BFF to update her on the situation.

"OMG! Tiffany, my meeting with the Bad Boyz has

turned into a HORRIFIC DISASTER! NO! They didn't tell me my DRESS was UGLY!! I'm totally GLAM and my lip gloss is poppin', but the Bad Boyz didn't even bother to show up! Not a single one of them. Tiffany, it was AWFUL! HOW am I supposed to get more followers on social media or start a juicy RUMOR that one of them is my BOYFRIEND if I can't get a SELFIE with any of them?! Tiff, my life is RUINED!!"

REALLY, MacKenzie?!! SORRY I'M NOT SORRY ☹!

I was just starting to get a little worried when I noticed something on the table near Trevor. . . .

OMG! IT WAS A BIRTHDAY MUFFIN ☹!!

Trevor was on his cell phone, trying to calm down the television producer. So I asked Mallory about the muffin.

"Well, it's kind of an inside joke, but that's the birthday muffin. Today is Nick's birthday, and we were going to give it to him and sing 'Happy Birthday' during our meeting!" Mallory explained.

"TODAY IS NICK'S BIRTHDAY?!!" I gasped.

"Yeah, unfortunately it's the same day as our big concert," Mallory said. "The whole thing started as a prank when Aidan gave Trevor a stale muffin as a birthday gift. And now it's kind of a tour tradition. It's silly, but it always gets a good laugh."

My head was SPINNING! Nick had mentioned something about a birthday muffin. And I had pretty much convinced him to celebrate his NEXT birthday with family and friends!

But when I said that, I had NO IDEA his birthday was ONLY a week away!

And on the same day as a huge televised concert!

Based on the magazines I had read, Nick was from New York City! Which meant his family and friends were in . . . OMG!!

If Nick missed this concert tonight because he was celebrating his birthday, it would be all MY fault ☹!!

I had a hunch where Nick was, but what about the other Boyz?!

I was trying to remember what I'd told each of them, when I noticed a television commercial. . . .

REFRESH
BOTTLED WATER
OFFICIAL SPONSOR OF
NYC REFRESH
SKATEBOARD EVENT SERIES
HOST: LATER SKATER PARK
MONDAY, JULY 28

That Refresh bottled water ad seemed really familiar. I was SURE I'd seen it somewhere . . . !

Then I remembered!

It was on the back of Aidan's SKATE MAGAZINE!!

The one he was READING when I told him it would be COOL to visit local SKATE PARKS!!

Aidan was probably at that Refresh skateboard event today. And it was all MY fault ☹!

Which meant it was MY fault that VICTOR was probably feeding SQUIRRELS in Central Park ☹!!

And also MY fault that Joshua was probably hanging out at the NEW YORK PUBLIC LIBRARY ☹!!

But what about their CONCERT tonight and their thousands of FANS?!

What if the Boyz ultimately decided they wanted to be normal guys, not famous pop stars?!

I was just trying to make them feel better when I gave them all that advice about being comfortable in their own skin and trying to enjoy life.

And I meant every word I said!

But what if I, Nikki Maxwell, was personally responsible for . . .

BREAKING UP the BAD BOYZ?!

MILLIONS of Bad Boyz fans around the world would HATE MY GUTS!

And I could instantly go from FAMOUS to INFAMOUS!

NOOOOOOOOO!!!

(That was me screaming!)

☹!!!

WEDNESDAY, JULY 30

Well, there was GOOD news and BAD news!

The good news was that the Boyz finally contacted Trevor around 4:00 p.m. by text and assured him that they were SAFE and PERFECTLY FINE! They were just mentally and physically exhausted, anxious, overwhelmed, frustrated, stressed out, irritable, and emotionally drained due to their grueling schedule for the past year.

And, as I had suspected, they had spent the day relaxing, hanging out, and doing what they enjoyed.

YES! Each of them had taken MY sound advice ☺!

I had helped the Boyz figure out what was really important to them, and that made ME feel like a wise, mature, and responsible young adult.

I was about to share this good news with Trevor when he sighed and shook his head in frustration as he complained to Mallory and his team.

"I know the Boyz are still young, but what they did was ridiculously IRRESPONSIBLE! We have millions of dollars invested in their careers and these concerts, and they can't just NOT show up whenever they FEEL like it!" he fumed.

That's when I suddenly decided maybe it WASN'T such a good idea to share that info with Trevor.

The bad news was that we weren't sure whether the Bad Boyz were going to show up for their NYC concert. We hadn't heard from them since their texts!

Trevor admitted that the situation was mostly his fault. "I don't know what's going to happen tonight, Nikki, but I've enjoyed having you and your band on this tour. And, to be honest, for the past two months the Boyz have been stressed out and fighting like cats and dogs! We were seriously considering rescheduling the last leg of our tour to give them a break so they could rest up a bit. But, unfortunately, it might be too late for that! I should have taken action to fix this problem a long time ago."

"Maybe it's NOT too late," I said. "Especially if you're willing to change their schedule so that the guys have a more balanced life."

"I agree." Trevor nodded. "The weird thing is that they've been getting along really well since your band joined the tour. You guys seem to have had a positive effect on them. I'm not exactly sure why. Anyway, it would be sad if tonight the Boyz broke up and went their separate ways. They're SUPERtalented and good kids. But, unfortunately, that's a real possibility!"

WILL THE BAD BOYZ BREAK UP ☹?!!

The GOOD NEWS was that Trevor was WRONG about the BAD NEWS!

The next morning it was all over the news, social media, and Hollywood gossip columns.

THE BAD BOYZ TOUR HAS BEEN CANCELED ☹!!

BUT ALL THE DATES ARE GOING TO BE RESCHEDULED AFTER THEY TAKE A MUCH-NEEDED BREAK FROM THEIR YEARLONG WORLD TOUR ☺!!

The announcement was made AFTER the Bad Boyz appeared and totally ROCKED their sold-out NYC CONCERT!! And, of course, my band, Actually, I'm Not Really Sure Yet, was their AWESOME opening act!

In spite of MacKenzie's EVIL plan, she wasn't able to CRASH our show and HOG the stage with her dance routines! And she NEVER, EVER got a chance to meet the Bad Boyz and claim that one of them was her boyfriend!

Mostly because I made SURE she NEVER, EVER got a BACKSTAGE PASS ☺! I didn't trust MacKenzie to hold up her side of the deal any farther than I could SPIT! I didn't believe she would help save Fuzzy Friends no matter WHAT we did, and I was so TIRED of her TERRORIZING us, I just LOST IT!

The NYC concert is going to be televised next week, and I can't wait to see it!

Anyway, I've been thinking about WHY the Bad Boyz stopped fighting once we joined the tour.

Especially since all I really did was listen to them, try to be supportive, and give them advice about the things they were struggling with.

Just like Chloe, Zoey, Brandon, and I all do for each other as BFFs.

That's when I finally figured it out!

What I had been for each of the Bad Boyz was . . .

A MUCH-NEEDED FRIEND ☺!

NOT a manager!

NOT a creative director!

NOT a support staff!

And NOT a superfan!

Well, okay!

I LIED!

I'm DEFINITELY a SUPERFAN!!

But STILL!!

☺!

THURSDAY, JULY 31

Chloe, Zoey, Brandon, Violet, Theo, Marcus, and I arrived back home from the Bad Boyz tour on Tuesday around noon ☺!

MacKenzie, too ☹! I still can't believe I actually SURVIVED having her as my ROOMMATE for ten very long, AGONIZING days!

I CRASHED and slept for, like, twenty-four hours straight! OMG! It was WONDERFUL to be back in my OWN bed again! With Brianna BANGING on my door, WHINING, and PESTERING me nonstop ☺!

Touring with the Bad Boyz was a lot of FUN! But it was also mentally and physically exhausting! Depending on how long a break they take, my band might finish the tour with them.

I already broke the news to MacKenzie that our little deal is OVER! I was like, GIRL, BYE!!

SORRY! But if she wants to audition for the

Bad Boyz, she's going to have to post a video online and get IGNORED just like everybody else!

In the meantime, I'm going to enjoy the rest of my summer and hang out with my BFFs and my crush. I can't believe school actually starts in less than FOUR weeks!

Brandon texted me with some really FANTASTIC news! His grandparents FINALLY received the new lease for the Fuzzy Friends building!

SQUEEEEEEE ☺!

Brandon said that he didn't find out until he got home, but the lease was actually sent earlier in the week, on Monday. About 3:30 p.m., to be exact.

It was actually around the time I was reading my letter to Trevor and about to BUST MacKenzie at that meeting. When she started freaking out and frantically texting someone, I thought it was Tiffany. But I was wrong! It must have been her dad! He sent that lease right over! And FAST!!

PROBLEM SOLVED ☺!

Anyway, Brandon stopped by and asked me if I wanted to HANG OUT!

He said that after touring with the Bad Boyz, he was now a huge fan and had just purchased their latest album. He asked if I wanted to listen to it with him.

Chloe and Zoey got me that album for my birthday, and I'd ALREADY heard it a thousand times!

But I decided NOT to mention any of those unimportant details to Brandon.

I told him, "YES!!" Then I very generously suggested that we share MY headphones!

What can I say?!

I'M SUCH A DORK!!

☺!!

ACKNOWLEDGMENTS

Ten years ago, I wrote a manuscript about a Dorky, insecure fourteen-year-old named Nikki J. Maxwell. In her diary, she chronicled her middle school adventures with over-the-top drama, a quirky sense of humor, and vivid illustrations. Never in my wildest dreams would I have ever imagined myself sitting here sixteen books later celebrating my ten-year anniversary with a cast of over fifty different Dork Diaries characters we've brought to life over the years!

None of this would have been possible without my SPECTACULAR editorial director, Liesa Abrams Mignogna. From day one you've been an inspiration to me, and I'm so happy to be on this writing journey with you! With each book, you've demonstrated your leadership and creativity and why you're the best in the business. I'm grateful to have you on Team Dork, and I'm thrilled that after ten years, I can still make you laugh out loud!

A special thanks to my SUPERtalented art director, Karin Paprocki. You can take a simple concept and transform it into a colorful masterpiece, setting the bar higher and higher with each book cover. You miraculously integrate text and artwork into a picture-perfect narrative, page after page, year after year!

To my AWESOME managing editor, Katherine Devendorf. Thanks for your expertise, attention to detail, and support in keeping us all on task through our editing process.

And a special thanks to Mara Anastas, who has been the compass that has steered this treasured series on a path toward continued success. Thank you for believing in Dork Diaries!

To Daniel Lazar, my BRILLIANT agent at Writers House. In 2009 you saw something special in me that I had yet to discover. And you knew I had created a compelling voice that would resonate with kids around the world. Today, I laugh at the thought that Nikki could have actually had a fairy godfather! Thank you for your friendship, BIG DREAMS, and unwavering support. I'm happy to celebrate this wonderful milestone with you and look forward to another ten years!

To my WONDERFUL Team Dork staff at Aladdin/Simon & Schuster, Rebecca Vitkus, Chriscynethia Floyd, Jon Anderson, Julie Doebler, Caitlin Sweeny, Anna Jarzab, Alissa Nigro, Lauren Hoffman, Nicole Russo, Lauren Carr, Jenn Rothkin, Ian Reilly, Christina Solazzo, Elizabeth Mims, Lauren Forte, Crystal Velasquez, Stephanie Voros, Amy Habayeb, Michelle Leo, Sarah Woodruff, Christina Pecorale, Gary Urda, and the entire sales force. Thanks for everything! You guys are remarkable and an author's dream.

A special thanks to my AMAZING Writers House family, including Torie Doherty-Munro and my foreign rights agents, Cecilia de la Campa and Alessandra Birch, for all of your hard work and dedication to the series. And to Deena, Zoé, Marie, and Joy, thanks for your help in making Dork Diaries so ADORKABLE!

To my INCREDIBLE daughter and PHENOMENAL illustrator, Nikki. Thank you for always being there for me. I could not have done this without you! I've watched you grow as an artist, and I'm SUPERexcited to see what you'll accomplish next! And to Kim, Doris, Arianna, and my entire family! Thanks for your unconditional love and support.

And last but not least, to my Dork Diaries superfans! Thanks for loving my book series. Always remember to let your inner DORK shine through!

Happy ten-year anniversary!!

SQUEEEE!!!!....

☺

PHOTOGRAPH © BY SUNA LEE

Rachel Renée Russell is the #1 *New York Times* bestselling author of the blockbuster book series Dork Diaries and the bestselling series The Misadventures of Max Crumbly.

There are more than forty-five million copies of her books in print worldwide, and they have been translated into thirty-seven languages.

She enjoys working with her daughter Nikki, who helps illustrate her books.

Rachel's message is "Always let your inner dork shine through!"

Do you love

and reading all about Nikki's not-so-fabulous life??

Then don't miss out on the BRAND NEW series from **Rachel Renée Russell!** featuring new dork on the block,

"If you like Tom Gates,
Diary of A Wimpy Kid and, of course,
Dork Diaries you'll love this!" *The Sun*

1. MY SECRET LIFE AS A SUPER~~HERO~~ ZERO

If I had SUPERPOWERS, life in middle school wouldn't be quite so CRUDDY.

Hey, I'd NEVER miss the stupid bus again, because I'd just FLY to school! . . .

AWESOME, right? That would pretty much make ME the COOLEST kid at my school!

But I'll let you in on a secret. Getting bombed by an angry bird is NOT cool. It's just . . . NASTY!!

TV, comic books, and movies make all this superhero stuff look SO easy. But it ISN'T! So don't believe the HYPE.

You CAN'T get superpowers by hanging out in a laboratory, mixing up colorful, glowing liquids that you simply DRINK. . . .

ME, MIXING UP A YUMMY SUPERPOWER SMOOTHIE

HOW do I Know it doesn't work? . . .

"OOPS!"

Let me put it this way. . . .

Even if I DID have superpowers, the very first person I'd need to rescue is . . .

MYSELF!

WHY?

Because a guy at school pulled a lousy PRANK on me.

And, unfortunately, I might be DEAD by the time you read this!

Yes, I said "DEAD."

Okay, I'll admit that he didn't MEAN to kill me.

But still . . . !!

So if you're the type who gets FREAKED OUT over this kind of stuff (or comic book cliffhangers), you probably shouldn't read my journal. . . .

Um . . . excuse me, but are you STILL reading?!

Okay, fine! Go right ahead.

Just don't say I didn't warn you!

2. IF THERE'S A DEAD BODY INSIDE MY LOCKER, IT'S PROBABLY ME!

It all started as a normal, boring, CRUMMY day in my abnormally boring, CRUMMY life.

My morning was a disaster because I overslept. Then it went straight downhill from there.

I completely lost track of time at breakfast while reading a really old comic book that my father found in the attic a few days ago.

He said his dad had given it to him as a birthday gift when he was a kid.

He warned me to be super careful with it and not take it out of the house because it was a collectible and probably worth a few hundred dollars.

My dad was pretty serious about it because he'd already scheduled an appointment to get it appraised at the local comic book store.

However, since I was running late for school, I decided to ~~sneak~~ take the comic book with me and finish reading it during lunch.

Like, what could happen to it at school?!

Anyway, as I rushed to the bus stop, the zipper broke on my backpack and all my stuff fell out, including Dad's comic book.

I was like, Oh, CRUD!! My dad is going to STRANGLE ME if I damage his comic book!

I grabbed the comic book and was desperately trying to pick up everything else when the bus pulled up, screeched to a halt, waited all of three seconds, and then zoomed off again.

Without me!

Hey, I ran after that thing like it was a $100 bill blowing in the wind!

"STOP!! STOP!! STOOOOP!" I yelled.

But it didn't.

Which meant I missed the bus, was forced to walk to school, and arrived twenty minutes late.

Next I got chewed out by the office secretary. She gave me a tardy slip and then threatened an after-school detention because I had interrupted her while she was eating a jelly doughnut.

And just when I thought things couldn't possibly get ANY worse, they did.

When I stopped by my locker to get my books, suddenly everything went DARK.

That's when I realized I was **TRAPPED** in my worst . . .

NIGHTMARE!

I Knew attending a new middle school was going to be tough, but this is INSANE.

My life STINKS!

I Know you're probably thinking, Dude, just chill! Everybody has a BAD day at school.

Stop whining and GET OVER IT!

For real?

Are you serious?

Like, HOW am I supposed to get over THIS?! . . .